To

Pamela Patterson

Love

Dermot O'Hanlon

16th March 2014

DAVID MADISON

By the same author

Ian Trevelyan, Book Guild Publishing, 2013

DAVID MADISON

The Scholarship Boy

Dermot O'Hanlon

Book Guild Publishing

Sussex, England

First published in Great Britain in 2014 by
The Book Guild Ltd
The Werks
45 Church Road
Hove, BN3 2BE

Typesetting in Baskerville by
Ellipsis Digital Ltd, Glasgow

Printed and bound in Great Britain by
CPI Group (UK) Ltd, Croydon, CR0 4YY

A catalogue record for this book is available from
The British Library.

ISBN 978 1 909716 07 0

To my
nephews and nieces
Redmond, Noëlle, Judy, Lucy, Leonard, Mark and Jim
Moira, Nuala, Róisín, Lorcan and Maeve
Rory, Gail and Jansis

Contents

1

David Recalls Some Past Events

David Madison was in bed early that fine September night, for the next day he was to enter St Donat's Abbey, a public school – a new chapter in his life which he was looking forward to with excitement, delight and, occasionally, fear. As he lay on his back, he recalled the flurry of events leading up to it. Mr McLeod, his teacher, was to be thanked for a great deal. It was this lean-faced Scot, with the burring brogue and the bright eyes of a zealot, who had suggested that he should do the scholarship examination in the first place.

'It's a braw school,' Mr McLeod had told his parents when he called on them, 'and the lad will never get a finer opportunity to show his capabilities. Aye, the competition will be very, very stiff – and there's only one place, mind ye – but I've great faith in the bairn, and the experience will no' come amiss later, whatever the result.'

When David heard what was afoot he was eagerness itself. Although it had meant curtailing most of his usual holiday activities in order to prepare for the examination in July, he set to work with a will; and, during the long, sunny days while his friends were making the welkin ring, he stuck doggedly at his books and worked along the lines Mr McLeod suggested. As he recalled the examination itself, a little smile played on his lips. All the twelve-year-olds in Lancashire seemed to have been crammed into that large hall with its myriad of single desks. A general air of suspicion was present since each boy was aware of the competition and suspected the unplumbed depths of a Euclid hidden behind the corrugated brows of his fellow candidates. While the majority refreshed their memories from notes and books in the intervals between papers, a few – the victims of misplaced confidence on the part of doting parents or foolish teachers – nonchalantly chewed sweets and cracked jokes with one another. On the whole, David liked the papers and acted upon the good counsel of Mr McLeod:

'There'll be no choice of questions so begin at number one on all the papers and work down in order. This will show the examiners that you have no special preferences, and since you won't end up with a weak answer because you've done your best ones first, your paper will be more balanced. Allow equal time for each question and leave plenty of space between your answers so that you can complete any unfinished ones or make additions to any of the others if you've got time to spare at the end. Finally, use diagrams and tabulate your facts where you can, as this saves valuable time.'

Mr McLeod also had him primed with many useful mnemonics, those little rhymes and phrases which are like rafts on a sea of uncertainty to overladen memories. Angus would not let him discuss the papers until the examination was finished. He explained that post-mortems usually revealed the inevitable mistakes and could lead to the inexperienced throwing in the towel in an otherwise equal fight. When it was over, Mr McLeod studied the questions with him and announced to his parents, brother Jack and sister Susan that 'David's done a bonny examination and he's a laddie to be proud of.' At which David flushed, both at hearing his own praise and seeing the evident pleasure of his parents.

Anxious days and weeks of waiting for the result followed. He spent a lot of time on his knees in church, but though he prayed for success he expected failure. However, realities and dreams are quite different things, and, lying in a half-sleep in bed each night before Jack came up to the bedroom, he would wonder what life was like at St Donat's. He saw visions of long ago when it had been inhabited by a community of monks, and he could almost hear the pealing of bells ringing out across the fields calling the brethren to prayer. He was sure that, although that was many centuries before, time could not erase all the old memories associated with the place, and that the abbot and his community would still seem to be present to the young and uncritical at heart. He knew that the Abbey (as the school was known) was in Essex, about twenty miles from Colchester, which Mr McLeod had told him had many historical associations with the early Britons and ancient Romans. He had never travelled outside the north of England and, to his boyish mind, the distance separating his home in Liverpool from St Donat's in East Anglia was not hundreds, but thousands of miles; and with his premonition of the result of the scholarship the Abbey might just as well have been situated on the moon. Then Jack would come up to bed and reality would reassert itself. If Jack thought that he was asleep, he would undress in the dark and steal quietly into bed. Otherwise, they would talk until conversational topics were exhausted and then drop off to sleep. David admired his much older brother, who seemed so full of worldly wisdom – wisdom that, though often voiced with more loudness than accuracy, passed muster in his opinion.

The letter which he had been waiting for so anxiously arrived at last. It was addressed to him, and he found it beside his plate one morning at breakfast. With trembling hands he opened it, but before he could finish reading the cruel information that it contained a catch came into his voice and his father took it from him and finished it for him. Although he had anticipated failure, the news still came as a shock; for this was the first time he had experienced how shattering an unsuccessful result can be. His mother patted him on the hand sympathetically, in all probability feeling his disappointment even more keenly than he did himself. After a short, speechless interval of disbelief, Jack exploded violently against examiners in general and the examination system in particular and muttered something about 'influence'.

Mr McLeod dropped in later in the morning and showed just as much annoyance over the result.

'If David were a wee Scot instead of a Lancastrian,' he told the family, 'I'd suspect a Sassenach plot to keep the scholarship among themselves.'

Angus began to call regularly after that, purportedly to keep them informed about his on-going considerations about whether he should question the result or not; but it was obvious to everyone that, since his first visit to the house about David early in the summer, he had begun to take an interest in Susan as well. David wondered just when he would ask her out.

The stimulating arrival of a second counter letter from the examining board forced his hand. This time the letter was addressed to David's father. It was one of apology and was in less formal language than the first had been. An error had been made in sending David an unsuccessful result, and this had been brought to light when his father had not written to accept the scholarship which he had won. The letter also said that Dr Princeton, the headmaster of St Donat's, would write later giving fuller details about the offer. Jack acknowledged the confession of the mistake with lordly understanding, admitting generously that he, too, sometimes made mistakes. Angus McLeod almost danced a Highland fling with delight and later, when he was alone with Susan, he spoke his piece.

'Now that the lad is settled, Susan, I won't have any further reason to call to the house except ...' He did not finish his sentence but went dourly about another approach. 'Will you come with me to the Royal Court on Saturday night to see a play?'

Susan had no real need to answer – although she did – for the look in her eyes was sufficient assent. She kissed David extremely affectionately that night, and since Jack didn't tease him about it David thought he knew why.

Dr Princeton wrote as promised and explained that the

scholarship included board, teaching and the provision of the required books for a period of six or so years, when David's secondary education would be completed.

David went on many thrilling shopping expeditions with his mother to buy the other requirements which his parents had to provide – two grey uniforms, a cap and blazer with the school's crest and colours, socks, ties, shirts, shoes, slippers, dressing gown, sports gear and dress, and a number of other odds and ends too numerous to mention. There was, of course, that standard piece of equipment for any self-respecting boarder – a sturdy boy-proof trunk. Each fresh addition to his wardrobe was a new delight, but David's most ecstatic moment was when his father painted his initials on the lid of the trunk.

At length, that drowsiness which is induced by the opiate of pleasant thoughts stole over David, and, with a smile on his face, he rolled over on his side and was soon in the arms of Morpheus.

2

Sir Frederick Voices his Disappointment

In the library of his home in Norfolk, Sir Frederick De Macey was talking earnestly with his wife about their son. In his hand, as a sort of indictment, was the latter's school report, and it was certainly not one to give comfort to any parent who was interested in his child's scholastic progress. His tone, as he spoke, was indicative of a mixture of disappointment and bewilderment.

'I can't understand it, but Richard is going from bad to worse in his studies and in his whole behaviour generally. He's a bitter disappointment to me, and I've never felt more humiliated in my life than I did yesterday. I think that just about summed up his attitude towards us.'

He was referring to an incident which had occurred the previous morning when Richard had informed them that he intended visiting a friend of his and, consequently, would not be home until late in the evening.

'Surely,' his father had commented, 'it's not too much to expect you to spend the last day of the holidays in your own home?'

'I promised Gilbert Roye that I'd call over' had been Richard's evasive reply, but he had then added in sullen compromise: 'But I'll be back about seven.'

'Very well, go if you must,' his father had said, trying to conceal how hurt he was. 'We don't intend to force you to stay here if you don't want to.'

A lot of sand would flow in the hourglass before time erased the bitter memory of that encounter with his son. Lady De Macey was equally upset but was able to cloak it better than her husband.

'You mustn't blame yourself, dear. You've always set him a fine example.'

'Being abroad so much and having to leave him with relatives so often has probably a lot to do with it. But what else could we do? Some of the places I've been posted to were completely unsuitable for one of his age. I sometimes wonder whether it was worth while sacrificing so much for so little return.'

Sir Frederick had been in the diplomatic service and had served in the four corners of the world. Richard had been left in the care of relatives who had, apparently, regarded his wilful disposition as something clever and amusing and had indulgently given him his head. His parents were now reaping the barren harvest of their laissez-faire attitude.

'You should have a talk with him before he leaves for school,' his wife advised. 'It might do some good.'

Her husband was not very sanguine about that hope.

'I doubt it. He's almost like a stranger to me and resents it if I show any concern about him.'

Richard came in and stood at the door. He was already dressed for the journey and was holding his school cap in his hands.

'Do you wish to see me before I go?' he asked in a well-modulated voice.

'Your father has a few things to say to you, Richard,' his mother answered, 'so I'll leave the two of you alone. You can see me in the garden later.' She went out, leaving father and son facing each other with an awkward uncertainty across the room.

'Please sit down, Richard,' Sir Frederick said with some embarrassment.

With evident reluctance, Richard did so. He was a very handsome boy, and his bearing and poise were excellent, but he was very petulant and self-willed. It affected his father deeply to watch him develop into a young, self-opinionated, headstrong – and it had to be faced – worthless type of person with few of the better qualities. Seeing his school report in his father's hand, Richard could not suppress a momentary, contemptuous smile.

'Are you happy at your present school?' his father inquired gruffly. He felt no sense of communion with his son, and it was quite true what he had told his wife – that they were almost on the same footing as strangers.

'Oh, the Abbey's all right. I've got a lot of friends there.'

'Won't you try and do better this term? Your last few reports have been very unsatisfactory, and the Headmaster is very dissatisfied with you.' Richard frowned and his face whitened a little with anger, but he said nothing. 'I asked you a question, Richard.'

'Everyone gets reports like that,' he said lamely and blushed at the lie.

'You seem to be making no progress whatsoever – and what's far worse, you don't even seem to be making any effort. Your mother and I are very unhappy, too, at the way you treat us. We never have much of your company, and we seldom see you except at mealtimes or when you want something. Tell me, do I know any of your school friends?'

'I couldn't say. Except Gilbert Roye,' he added as an after-thought.

'The manufacturer's son?'

'Yes.'

Sir Frederick recalled a loud, unpleasant, smug-faced boy who was the spoiled offspring of equally unpleasant parents.

'He doesn't strike me as being the type of boy you should associate with.'

'You don't know him like I do!' came the hot but logical retort.

'Perhaps I don't.' Rightly supposing that any further such references to this particular friend of his son's might undo whatever small good his talk might have, his father dismissed him from the conversation. 'However, Richard, take my advice and choose your companions wisely. Worthwhile friends who can influence you for the good are an inestimable blessing.'

Richard shifted his feet petulantly, thereby conveying the impression that such remarks should be confined to children much younger than himself.

'I'll have to go now if I'm to catch my train.'

'You could get one later. Better still, I could drive you to St Donat's myself.' That way, he thought, he could then continue the talk with his son on the way and perhaps get closer to him.

But Richard stood firm.

'I promised Gilbert that I'd meet him at the station.'

His father went over to him and put his hands on his shoulders.

'Remember what I've just said,' he told him, but his son didn't reply. He kissed him on the forehead and felt him draw away as if instinctively. 'Goodbye, Richard.'

'Goodbye.' Richard put on his cap and, without further ado, turned on his heel and walked out of the room.

Sir Frederick sat down as if weary. He was both disappointed and humiliated by his son's attitude during their talk. With another father and son the parting would have been a moment of tenderness, but to Richard it meant only that another school year was about to begin.

3

David Enters the Public School

The Madisons were early astir on David's last morning at home. David himself was up with the lark and was feeling so excited that he hardly knew whether he was standing on his head or on his heels. He scarcely touched his breakfast apart from drinking half a cup of tea and eating a slice of toast.

'Aren't you feeling well, David?' his mother asked solicitously, busily scanning his face for signs of sickness. He was quite a good-looking boy, with dark-brown hair neatly fringed in front and deep-blue eyes which were now shining like stars at the prospect of the journey ahead. But his complexion was as glowing as ever with no telltale paleness or flushing to be detected.

'No, Mum,' he answered with a smile. 'I just don't feel like eating this morning, that's all.'

She then put his lack of appetite down to excitement, and her husband, knowing that she would like to see him eat a good meal before setting out, suggested a solution.

'David can have breakfast on the train later, Mother. I'm sure he'd enjoy that.' There was a twinkle in his eye as he said this, and Jack and Susan laughed.

'Goodbye, young 'un!' Jack said before leaving for work, putting a couple of pound notes in his jacket pocket. 'Let's hear from you soon.'

David thought that he detected a note of sadness in his brother's voice, but perhaps it was only because he himself felt sad about leaving his brother. When the taxi, which had been ordered the night before, came to take them to Lime Street Station, his mother made sure that he was well buttoned up – for it was still early in the morning and there was a sharpness in the air. With the help of a porter, his father put his precious trunk in the guard's van.

The three travellers were barely in their compartment when the train, with a loud warning shriek, departed for London and was soon clanking over the points of the intervening stations. David had breakfast in the dining car and watched the fields and countryside go swiftly by as he ate. It was a new experience to eat while travelling, and one which he enjoyed with full boyish enthusiasm. He had never seen so many trains in his life as they whooshed by from the opposite direction. This being the mid-1950s, he tried to guess whether their engines were steam-powered or the newer diesel-powered locomotives that were replacing them.

In London they took a train in Liverpool Street Station for the final stage of their journey into East Anglia, and in the late after-noon they reached the small market town of Abbeymead in Essex.

The small platform of the station was alive with boys of various ages and sizes who were returning from their holidays. Noise, tumult and pandemonium reigned supreme, shouts and laughter blended in the air, and confusion was the order of the day. Some of the boys were dressed in quiet grey uniforms, others wore caps and blazers in the Abbey's colour of red with braid trimming, while an occasional duffel coat was to be seen which made the wearer as conspicuous as a bohemian in a gathering of clergymen. Besides the ubiquitous trunk, every conceivable size and shape of box, case and container found its way on to the platform. Boys were looking for strayed posses-sions; parents were looking for strayed boys. Porters were trundling barrows of baggage outside the station to waiting taxis and cars, followed by their owners. Friend greeted friend like long-lost brothers. When David and his father managed to get the trunk off the train safely, his mother asked a boy who was about his own age the way to the school.

Although he had still some years to go before his voice broke, the boy answered the question with an adolescent hoarseness: 'It's about a mile from the town on the main road.' He inspected the party through horn-rimmed spectacles, and then turned his attention to the trunk. 'You'll need a taxi to take *that* along,' he advised, pointing at it, and they took his advice.

Their first view of St Donat's Abbey was breathtaking. As the taxi rounded a bend in the road, its church and clock towers appeared above the surrounding trees, its grey masonry and slated roofs blending pleasantly with the many greens of the luxuriant foliage which surrounded the building. Gradually, the full aspect of the Abbey was revealed in all its medieval magnificence.

On their arrival at the main building, they were directed to the study of the Headmaster, Dr Princeton, who greeted them warmly. He had a very special word of praise for David, telling them that he was proud to have him as a pupil and how brilliantly he had done in the examination. While he was speaking about him, he kept viewing him with his steady, steel-grey eyes which seemed to pierce into the depths of his soul.

He was the most imposing person David had ever seen. He was tall and, although a scholar, his back was as straight as a lance. He had a strong, purposeful face, and the set of his lips did much to betray whatever frame of mind he was in at any particular time. A wisp of curling grey hair tended to soften his physical cragginess and suggested that he was essentially paternal in nature. His handshake had been firm and friendly, but all the same David did his best to stay in the background.

Dr Princeton then conducted them around the beautiful building and recounted something of its history. David hadn't been far wrong when he had surmised what it would be like. Originally, it had been a pre-Reformation abbey. It was built in the Gothic architectural style and was covered in ivy where the older walls remained. The quadrangle still retained the ancient name of Cloister Court, and this was connected to Great Cloister, while a Cloister Passage gave access to Abbot's House, the house in which David would have his dormitory and study. After their tour they met Mrs Princeton, the Headmaster's wife, a very warm person who also had a lot of nice things to say about David. Soon after this, his parents took their leave, and he could hardly hold back his tears when they kissed him goodbye.

When they had gone, a terrible void filled his heart and an intense loneliness overcame him. How friends were to be made without some sort of introduction baffled him. Most of the boys were in pairs or groups, or else with their parents, and except for odd glances of curiosity in his direction no one seemed to be very interested in him. He saw a big, flashy American car pull up on the drive, and he watched as two boys and a man got out. The latter was an unpolished mountain of fleshy arrogance who puffed stertorously as he levered himself out of the driving seat. The likeness to him of one of the boys was very obvious – pimply of face and flabby of body, complacent in his manner and loud-voiced in his talk, he bore all the signs of being as unpleasant an individual as his parent.

The other boy was Richard De Macey. He had lied to his father about returning to school by train and had previously accepted an invitation from his friend, Gilbert Roye, to go in Mr Roye's car. David was not so sure about this other new arrival as he was about the other and he smiled at him as they came near. Richard, however, looked straight through him. Gilbert whispered something in Richard's ear, and they both laughed as they passed him, so, presumably, they were sharing some joke at his expense. David was hurt and blushed crimson, resolving to make no more friendly overtures unless he was encouraged to do so first. This show of unfriendliness made his sense of loneliness more acute, and to avoid any further embarrassments he kept well out of the way of the other boys.

4

David Makes New Friends

Dr Princeton came into the Common Room of Abbot's House where one of his masters was standing at the window looking at the boys and their parents strolling about the grounds.

'I've been around the other houses, Mr Ledwidge,' Dr Princeton said, 'and I've left Abbot's until last, as usual. Have all the new boys arrived yet?'

Mr Ledwidge was a slightly stooped old man with a quiet and serene manner. After a short, leisurely search, he took a slip of paper out of one of his pockets and perused it through reading glasses.

'I've accounted for all I'm expecting, Headmaster, except for young Madison. I haven't come across him so far.' He handed the paper to the Headmaster who inspected it at arm's length. It was a list of the new pupils who were coming to Abbot's House, and, save for David's name, all the others had a tick mark opposite them.

'He came with his parents about an hour ago. I was disappointed not to find you here when I was showing them around. I would have liked them to meet you. Madison is a brilliant boy and I'm quite sure that he'll avail himself of the scholarship to the full. I wish that all the boys coming here were only half as good.'

The old man smiled.

'Abbot's has got its usual quota of frightened newcomers. I always marvel at the fact that, since their applications for admission date from birth, so many of them have survived so long.'

'They're coming to the right house,' observed the Headmaster laughing, 'and will soon settle down. The younger boys, I'm afraid, who come into little contact with me, consider me to be a kind of Caligula or, at best, a benevolent despot. I think the majority of them have as their goal to pass through the school without ever crossing my path. At times, their efforts to avoid me are laughable.'

'Since it's usually something serious which brings them before you, I suppose they associate you with Nemesis.'

'You're probably right.' The Headmaster became serious in mien. 'I've had a letter from Sir Frederick De Macey about his son. He's very concerned about him.'

Mr Ledwidge removed his glasses and twirled them thought-fully in the air.

'I'm very concerned about him myself, Headmaster. With the best will in the world, I couldn't bring myself to soft-pedal in my term report. It was a stiff one for any parent to read, but Sir Frederick appreciates frankness. He realizes that ignoring his son's deficiencies and pretending they're not there will solve nothing. Apart from scholastic matters, De Macey leaves plenty to be desired in many other ways, too. His natural intelligence is unquestionable, but he shows no inclination to interest himself in his work. His whole attitude needs reorienting or he'll end up a hopeless case.'

'After what you've just said, I'd say that your report was more charitable than it could have been.'

'He's unpopular with most of the other boys and that's a very bad sign. Usually, unpopularity is a well-earned distinction, if one can call it that.'

'He'll have to pull up his socks and face up to things or he'll be thrown on life's scrap heap. Can you suggest a remedy?'

'I don't know,' Mr Ledwidge replied, shaking his head. 'He's as headstrong and as self-opinionated as the boys he goes about with. I think one of the roots of the trouble lies there. However, one thing is sure – he's not a boy to be driven and coercive measures in any form would certainly fail.'

'I suppose it's inevitable that a few of our boys should fall by the wayside.'

'Yes, unfortunately.'

Just then, David came into the Common Room. He was alone and looking a bit lost; so far he had failed to find the encouragement he needed to strike up a friendship or at least to speak to some of the other boys. When he saw the two masters he shyly tried to make a retreat, but Dr Princeton called after him.

'Don't go, Madison,' he said. 'This is the clever little boy whom you've been missing, Mr Ledwidge.'

The old man smiled at David.

'I'm pleased to meet you, Madison. I'm sure we'll get along well together, won't we?'

'Yes, sir,' David replied in a small voice.

'You won't be long making friends here. This is a friendly house. Have you met any of the other boys yet?'

'Not yet, sir.' In his heart of hearts he doubted if he ever would.

'Never mind. Abbot's may appear deserted at the moment, but it won't be for long.'

The Headmaster laughed.

'I presume that news has already gone over the school grapevine that I'm on the premises. I'll be watching your progress closely, Madison. I'm expecting great things of you.'

'Thank you, sir!'

The Headmaster and Mr Ledwidge left the room, discussing the curriculum for the year as they went out. With his hands behind his back, David began to inspect the room and examined the photographs and records of the scholastic and athletic achievements of past and present residents of Abbot's House which lined the walls.

Two boys, similarly dressed to himself in grey school uniforms, came in laughing. He recognized one of them as the boy who had directed them at the station, but the other he hadn't seen before. As lively as a cricket, the latter was about his own age and height, but was slighter and less robust in build. His hair was brown and, like his own, fringed in front, and in a palish face, which was scarred on one cheek, glowed large, lustrous, brown eyes. Neither of them had seen him yet, and David hoped that he would remain unnoticed as he pretended to be absorbed in his scrutiny of one of the photographs.

'That was a close shave, Arthur,' laughed the vivacious one gleefully. 'A second sooner and we'd have bumped into the Doctor. Did you see the way he looked at me, as if I'd already been up to some mischief?'

His companion uttered a few hoarse chuckles.

'You have a morbid fear of him, Tony. You only imagined it.'

'Perhaps I did, but I can tell you that I'll give him a wide berth this term. I won't run too many risks where *he*'s concerned.'

'He's got a heart of gold and you'd be the first to admit it.'

'I suppose so.'

'I'm glad you're back. The place would be as dead as a wake without you.'

Arthur looked about the room. He saw David and came over to him. 'Hello! I saw you at the station. You're a new boy, aren't you?'

David was a bit on the defensive, but answered with a shy smile: 'Yes. My name's Madison – David Madison.'

'I'm glad to know you. I'm Arthur Gillespie.' David almost breathed audibly with relief when he saw that no snubs or insults were intended. 'This is Tony Masefield.'

Tony came from behind Arthur where he had retreated, suddenly subdued, as soon as he had noticed the stranger. They all shook hands and Tony again retreated into the background.

Arthur chuckled at this. 'He's not always as quiet as this,' he told David. 'Are you, Tony?'

The other smiled charmingly and shook his head.

'No, Arthur.'

'You'll probably be in our class, David. Where do you come from?'

'From Liverpool.'

'I was in Lancashire once when I was young, but I don't remember it. I like Lancashire hotpot, though.'

David was now more at his ease. However, he sensed that Tony Masefield was weighing him up with those lustrous brown eyes of his, and he wondered what kind of an impression he was making on him.

'Do you come from far away, Arthur?' he asked in his turn.

'I live between here and Abbeymead. I'm the only day boy in Lower School. At the moment I'm waiting for my father to drive me home. He's a GP and the doctor who visits here. I should be with him now helping him with the medical supplies for sickbay, but I suppose he and Matron will be able to manage without me. It's really Tony's fault. I wouldn't be here if it wasn't for him.'

Tony was still quiet but he had come from behind Arthur now.

'That's a good excuse for not helping, Arthur.' For the first time, he directly addressed the newcomer. 'I live in Suffolk. Our house is just outside a small village.'

'Tony's being uncharacteristically modest, David. He lives near Masefield, a village founded by an ancestor of his donkey's years ago for his workers, and his home is Masefield Manor, which has about a hundred rooms.'

'You're exaggerating, Arthur,' Tony said, but admitted, a little less modestly, 'though it does have a lot of rooms. When I was little more than a toddler I got lost in the place one day and they couldn't find me for hours. I was always very venturesome, unlike good old dependable, stick-in-the-mud Arthur here. But it's not always a bed of roses living in a big house. In winter most of the rooms are unheated and are as cold as ice and it's like living in Siberia. How did you like Dr Princeton, David?'

'He was very nice, but he made me feel uncomfortable.'

'He affects us all like that,' commented Arthur hoarsely. 'He's a decent sort, though, and doesn't interfere if he can avoid it. If you're ever on the mat before him, David, you're for it.'

'That seldom happens,' added Tony in qualification.

'Why, Arthur? Does he cane the unlucky ones?'

'No, David,' Tony cut in before the other could reply. 'There's really no one kinder, but that's where it hurts. I'd rather take six of the best than one of his lectures.'

Arthur chuckled.

'You should know, Tony. You were up before him last term.'

'What happened?' David asked interestedly.

'Oh, it was nothing really,' was the apparently casual reply.

Arthur was highly amused at his feigned reticence about disclosing the reason.

'He's itching to tell you about it, David. Aren't you, Tony?'

'Don't listen to him, David,' Tony replied, laughing. He had evidently decided that he liked the newcomer and was warming up. 'He's only jealous because it didn't happen to him. See this scar?' He pointed to the scar on his cheek with a note of pride in his voice.

David inspected it.

'Yes. It's pretty big.'

'Six inches long at least.'

'It's only a nick,' Arthur observed disparagingly. 'How it has lasted so long is a freak of pathology.'

'I distinctly remember your father saying that it was an eight-degree incision, or something like that. Anyway, David, last term I climbed up into the clock tower. The view from the top is terrific. But I almost forgot about the chimes. If they rang while you were up there you'd be driven crazy. I had only a minute to spare before they chimed the hour, and coming down I slipped on one of the steps and a pencil in my top pocket ripped my cheek.'

'He could easily have broken his neck,' Arthur commented.

'That was only one of my nine lives, Arthur. The clock tower's out-of-bounds, of course, and some sneak reported me. Dr Princeton read the Riot Act to me and then sent me to Matron for a dressing.'

'My father was with Matron at the time and made the alleged statement about the wound,' said Arthur, winking at David.

Tony laughed.

'You needn't believe me if you don't want to. Dr Princeton makes you feel that you've let him down, David, and that hurts more than any cane or lecture.'

'I'll do my best to stay out of his way then,' David promised fervently.

'By the way, Tony, isn't there an empty bed beside yours in the dormitory?' Arthur asked, cleaning his glasses with a cloth which he had taken out of their case.

'Yes. There's another empty one almost opposite as well. Why?'

'David can sleep beside you.'

'Thanks, Arthur,' David said gratefully, marvelling at his good fortune in having someone to see that he got settled in properly.

Tony clicked his tongue in annoyance because he had missed the obvious.

'I never thought of that. It's a smashing idea.'

'I'll fix up with Matron about the bed,' Arthur said. 'I can twist her around my little finger.'

Heavy footsteps could be heard coming down the corridor towards the room long before anyone appeared. A fat, jolly, bespectacled man rushed in energetically as if he hadn't a moment to lose. David guessed immediately that he and his friend Arthur were father and son.

'I've been looking for you all over the place, Arthur,' he said, mopping his perspiring brow with a spotted handkerchief. 'I was very nearly going home without you. Hello, Tony! How are you after the holidays?'

'Fit as a fiddle, Doctor.'

'You could do with a few more roses in your cheeks,' Dr Gillespie commented, chucking him under the chin.

Tony laughed merrily.

'I'm the stringy type. I'll outlive the lot of you.'

'That was a nasty wound you got last term. I hope you'll keep out of the clock tower in future.'

'You'll give him a complex about his scar, Father,' Arthur said, grimacing jocosely at David. 'This is David Madison. He's new here.'

'How do you do, David!' The doctor shook David's hand vigorously and laughed jovially. 'You shouldn't be getting into such bad company so soon. They'll soon show you the ropes. Arthur's not over-brainy at bookwork, but he's very precocious for his age. I think he knows more about medicine than I do. Bring David over for tea later, Tony. Come along, Arthur – we'll let your mother know that they'll be coming.' With a cheery wave of his hand he steered his son out of the room.

'We'll get lots to eat, David,' Tony exulted rapturously. 'Arthur's mother is a terrific cook.'

'It was kind of him to invite us.'

'This won't be the last time either. There's always a great welcome there. Is this your first time away from home?'

'Yes.'

'You'll be homesick at first, but you'll get over it quickly enough. The first night in a strange bed is the worst. A good tuck-in at Arthur's will keep you from thinking too much about it for a while.'

'When do we go there?'

Tony looked at his watch.

'In about an hour's time. We can unpack our things before we go so that we won't have to rush back to do it. Is that all right with you, David?'

'That suits me, Tony.'

They went upstairs to the dormitory where they found the school porter sorting out a small mountain of trunks and suitcases.

'It's good to see you again, Master Tony,' the porter said.

'Charlie's full of blarney, David,' Tony commented laughing. 'I bet he says that to all the boys.'

Charlie shook his grizzled old head in stolid correction.

'Not all of 'em. The missus says that a bloomin' reformatory would be more fittin' for some of 'em. You know that, Master Tony.'

'We have some of them in Abbot's,' replied Tony, nodding in agreement.

'You're right there, and no mistake.'

'This is a new pupil, Charlie – David Madison.'

Under wrinkled brows the porter studied the newcomer with his bright little eyes.

'I'm right pleased to make your acquaintance, Master David. And if I may say so, you couldn't wish for a better mate. I knew his father, too. Good stock breeds true, I always say.'

'You're a blatherskite, Charlie,' Tony said, pleased with what he had said. 'But if you must talk, why not tell David about the Abbot?'

Charlie gave David a sidelong, scrutinizing glance.

'It's a bit soon for that.'

'Oh go on, tell him.'

'I don't know. Perhaps it would be better to wait until he's sort o' settled in.'

'Go ahead,' Tony persisted. 'He can take it.'

'All right, if you insist, Master Tony.'

Charlie sat down on a chair and, after a dramatic pause, began his story.

'You know that this here St Donat's was a real abbey once?' he asked, addressing David, who nodded affirmatively. 'Now I'm not trying to frighten you, Master David, and I've never seen anything myself, mind you, but there are some as say that the Abbot ain't where dead abbots ought to be.'

His young listeners were enthralled and Tony's eyes were wide with fearful delight, although he must have heard the tale scores of times before.

'Ain't where he ought to be, they say. This here was his house before he, ah' – Charlie groped dramatically for the appropriate word – 'disappeared. They say he didn't die natural-like and still haunts the Abbey.'

'Has anyone ever seen him, Charlie?' inquired David anxiously.

'Not as I've heard, Master David. But I wouldn't be found dead in Abbot's House after dark even if they were to make me king of England, Manchuria and Outer Mongolia!' He put mounting emphasis on each place and was on his feet at the last. He knew how to tell a story and understood the value of a little light relief at the end to allay his listeners' fears.

The boys laughed and, although David had been a bit alarmed by what Charlie had told them, the humorous ending seemed to put the seal of fiction on it. At least, so he tried to convince himself. After unpacking, he and Tony went to Arthur's house for tea. Tony had not been exaggerating, and Mrs Gillespie, as good-humoured and jolly a person as her husband, gave them a bumper home-cooked meal, and they ate like young horses till boyish stomachs could hold no more. When they had eaten, Arthur showed them his collection of stamps and cigarette cards. Tony had seen them dozens of times before, but he was just as interested as if he had never done so, for his capacity to summon up enthusiasm at will was enormous. Arthur then brought them into his father's consulting room and impressed them by taking their blood pressures – at least, he said he did.

That night in the dormitory before they got into bed, Tony, regarding David fixedly, remarked in a very serious tone of voice during a break in their conversation: 'I like you, David, and I'm glad we met today as we did. We'll have lots of fun together, and tomorrow I'll introduce you to all of my friends.'

That made David very happy. When the lights were switched off, he lay awake long after Tony had gone to sleep. That empty feeling of loneliness, which he had experienced after his parents had left for home, had returned with renewed force. Still, he was happy, for the first day in the Abbey had given him two good friends.

5

David Settles Down

As he had promised, Tony introduced David to his friends, who received him into their company with open arms. David rapidly showed his superiority in class and within a few weeks was acknowledged the best in his form. His love of learning was deep, and the new vistas that were opened up by the Latin and Greek languages delighted him. Mr Ledwidge began to show a great interest in him, for it was a pleasure to impart knowledge to such a willing and retentive mind. At games, too, David was among the best, and he had already been noted by Thornley, the Lower School Captain, as a valuable sports' asset. Since he was always ready to assist the halt and the lame, both in class and on the playing field, he soon earned a well-deserved popularity.

Arthur and Tony became his special friends. Tony, being a boarder, was particularly attached to him, and they were seldom out of each other's sight. Quarrels, so common in boyhood among close companions, never arose between them. Arthur, so adult in his thoughts and ways, was too sober and emotionally stable to allow any friction in their friendship; while David, with his even temper and a deep sense of consideration for others, rarely quarrelled with anyone. Surprisingly enough, the ebullient, excitable Tony never fought or fell out with his other friends either, although his quick temper frequently landed him in hot water in other quarters. If all the disputes in which he had engaged had come to blows, he wouldn't have lasted a term in the school. The three sat side by side in class on one of the back benches. Behind them was a large window which gave a commanding view of the school grounds, and David liked looking towards the playing fields where the groundsman was often to be seen at work. Mr Ledwidge occasionally noticed him in a half-turned attitude, but never rebuked him for it.

One afternoon, before Mr Ledwidge arrived for lessons, the boys were chatting and laughing gaily and indulging in the usual high-spirited horseplay about the classroom. Tony was sitting astride the sill of the open window, while David and Arthur were speaking to him from their bench. The master entered suddenly and he jumped smartly into his place and was beside his friends when the class rose respectfully to its feet.

'Sit down, boys,' Mr Ledwidge commanded kindly, eyeing them as if to say that he knew them all too well for the wool to be pulled over his eyes. He put a pile of exercise books on his table and then began to throw them one by one to their owners, commenting upon them as he did so. '"Hunting Song" was written by Sir Walter Scott, Thornley, not Sir Walter Raleigh.' The boy he was addressing was a placid, easy-going type, whose sturdy build was somewhat camouflaged by long trousers. 'I got your list of players for the rugger. I see that you've changed Masefield out to the wing and put Madison into his place. That's a good move. His speed will stand him in good stead there and he'll be less likely to run into so much trouble with that hot temper of his where he has more space. Madison is better suited both temperamentally and in build for defence work.'

'That's why I've changed them, sir. I've tried them out in their new positions and they couldn't be better.'

Mr Ledwidge smiled.

'Good! Last year I was afraid that sooner or later Masefield would get himself massacred. At times, his combative spirit blinds him to the folly of unequal combat.'

'I survived all the same, sir,' Tony said delightedly. He was thrilled by this fortuitous publicity.

'Miracles still happen, Masefield, miracles still happen,' observed the old man, beaming at him. He threw an exercise book to Gilbert Roye who was sitting beside Richard De Macey and a few more of his cronies at the back of the class on one of the other benches. 'Remember, Roye,' he warned, 'i before e, except after c.' Gilbert reddened angrily and glowered impotently with lowered head. 'We may use English letters in writing Latin, De Macey, but we still use Latin words.'

'Yes, sir,' replied Richard sullenly.

'You keep repeating the same mistakes over and over again. Do try to be more careful in future. The notes I write in your exercise books are for your own good. "From *nemo* let me never say *neminis* and *nemine*", Masefield. When your father was here I had to check him for the same Classical mistake. Perhaps it's hereditary. Still, you're showing a distinct improvement. I hope you're not looking over Madison's shoulder too often?'

Tony laughed.

'Not too often now, sir.'

'Well, keep it up.' Arthur received his copy next. 'If your father used the same kind of Latin in his prescriptions as you do, Gillespie, his patients would be taking a chance. There's little I can say about your work, Madison,' he told David, 'except that you rarely make a mistake.'

'Thank you, sir.'

'Are you sure you haven't done Latin before?'

'No, sir. I mean, yes, sir.' David was confused by the negative in the question.

Mr Ledwidge smiled.

'I take it you haven't, eh?'

'No, sir, not until I came here.'

'You've made remarkable progress at it. I wish there were more Classical scholars in the class like you.'

There was a sudden commotion in one corner of the room. A bird had flown in through the open window and alighted on the bench occupied by Roye and De Macey. Anxious to draw

26

attention to himself, Roye stood up and called excitedly to the master: 'Sir, sir, there's a sparrow in the room.'

Mr Ledwidge turned slightly in his direction and answered: 'Well, Roye, what do you expect for your school fees? A blooming eagle?'

The remark caused a general roar of merriment, and even Richard De Macey smiled, although the joke was against his friend, who sat down blushing furiously. Class ended and the boys began to troop out of the room. Mr Ledwidge rose from his chair to follow, but before reaching the door he stopped abruptly and passed a hand across his eyes. He steadied himself against the jamb with the other and returned to his table and sat down weakly on his chair.

Showing great concern, David, who was still in the room, hurried over to him.

'Is there anything wrong, sir?' he inquired, his eyes full of concern. 'Can I get you anything?'

'I'll be all right in a minute, Madison,' the master replied after a short pause. 'But it's very thoughtful of you to ask.' He was deeply touched by the boy's obvious solicitude. He stood up and, after steadying himself for a moment or two, left the room.

'I hope nothing happens to him,' David said to his friends.

Tony laughed at his fears.

'Nothing will ever happen to Mr Ledwidge, David. The school just couldn't carry on without him. Tell me,' he went on, changing the subject, 'what in the name of Caesar's aunt do you say instead of *neminis* and *nemine*?'

'*Nulli* and *nullo*.'

'We can't all expect to be geniuses like you,' Tony commented with a wry grimace. 'But such a stupid thing! Telling what you're *not* to say instead of what's right. The people who write the grammars must be barmy.'

Mr Ledwidge was forgotten. Tony had been so definite about his indestructibility that David stopped worrying about him.

6

The Unpleasantness Begins

For David, the first month in his new school was a happy one and passed uneventfully, and in his long letters home he recorded his little experiences and described St Donat's and its school life as graphically as he could. In October, when the evenings were drawing in, and the weather was becoming cold but exhilarating, the school grapevine – once mentioned by Dr Princeton as the source of important information in the school – suddenly buzzed with the news that he had a scholarship, a fact hitherto kept hidden from his peers. He wondered apprehensively what difference this would make when his friends got to hear about it. He needn't have worried, for, if anything, they were a little awed by his scholastic triumph and admired him all the more for it. In certain quarters, however, the information was mulled over in the minds of those boys who had come to hate him because of his ever-growing popularity and who now awaited their chance to turn it to their advantage. The opportunity they had been waiting for eventually presented itself. One night in the Common Room, Tony was plying him with question after question about his family. He wanted to know what his father and Jack worked at, what Susan did, and about his old Highland master, Angus McLeod. David could hardly keep up with his interested queries but did his best to cope with them. He was proud of his family and it was like being home again talking about them. The conversation slowly veered round to schoolwork, and Thornley, who had joined them, aired a generally held opinion.

'You're a snip to win all the prizes at the end of the year, David. None of us will get so much as a sniff at them.'

'Listen to him!' cried Tony in mock disgust. 'Handing out compliments to one of the newest in Abbot's, while at the same time he kicks the old warhorse out to the wing.' He was referring, of course, to the Captain altering his own position in the rugby team. 'I've a good mind never to play for St Donat's again, Thornley.'

Thornley smiled good-naturedly.

'You must admit you were a bit reckless in your old position. You were a constant worry to me.'

Tony almost exploded.

'Reckless? It'll be a sad day for the school when the Captain has to nursemaid me. There's not a player from Land's End to John o' Groat's who isn't afraid of me, David. I've brought down every forward in the country. You won't get my vote for Lower School Captain next time, Thornley.'

'If my decision helps to keep you in the land of the living, Tony, I'll be satisfied,' the Captain laughed, sitting down at one of the tables and beginning to read.

'Bookworm! By the way, David, the scholarship exam must have been a corker.'

'It wasn't too bad. I was lucky, that's all.'

'Don't be modest! There must have been an awful crowd in for it, but I'm glad you got it. The school wouldn't be the same without you. But you don't look the studious type, and I work harder than you do. You just seem to lap it up.'

David smiled at him.

'I've got a good memory, Tony. It just comes naturally.'

'I wish it was like that with me,' Tony said enviously. 'For every ounce of knowledge I get I lose a gallon of sweat. If I had to pass an exam like that to come here, I'd never have managed it in a hundred years. Arthur says that I was born with a silver spoon in my mouth.' He smiled engagingly. He seemed a bit ashamed of the fact that he had been born into most things.

It was at this moment that David got a foretaste of the unpleasantness to come.

'I didn't know we had a scholarship boy in the school, Richard,' Gilbert Roye remarked. He and De Macey and some of their satellites had been listening intently to all that had passed between David and his friend. His oafish voice carried across the room and a sudden silence fell, a silence that was broken only by a few encouraging sniggers from his set.

'Neither did I, Gilbert,' Richard remarked, smiling, in a voice as taunting as the other's. 'He shouldn't be let into a school like St Donat's.'

Roye smirked all over his pudgy face.

'If my parents knew about it, they'd probably take me away.'

'Shut up, you two,' Thornley told them, looking up from his book. 'You shouldn't be eavesdropping.'

Gilbert ignored him and continued with his biting insults.

'Any riff-raff can pass an exam, but they shouldn't expect us to mix with them.'

'At least he knows his place,' Richard observed provokingly. 'He doesn't try to deny it.'

'Have you anything to say, Madison?' jeered Roye, looking in David's direction.

But David held his peace. The first heartless words had struck him like a thunderbolt and he was blushing with embarrassment and indecision. He didn't quite know how to handle the situation and needed time to think things over, so he gritted his teeth and said nothing. But he hadn't bargained for Tony. A little colour had come into the latter's pale cheeks and the veins stood out angrily like blue cords in his neck.

'David wouldn't lower himself to speak to the likes of you. He has more brains in his little finger than you and De Macey put together.'

'We weren't talking about you, Masefield,' Richard exclaimed angrily, 'so you keep out of it.'

David tried to restrain him but Tony's blood was at boiling point.

'Roye has never had anything to boast about,' he cried shrilly. 'Everyone in the school knows that his father went about the country collecting rags before he began to manufacture thrash for hucksters.'

There was a general laugh at Tony's fluent invective, which found its mark through a chink in Roye's armour. Gilbert was livid with rage.

'How dare you, you skinny little blighter!'

'Let Madison fight his own battles,' Richard advised threateningly.

'Tony …' began David, making another attempt to restrain him, but it would have been easier to stop a runaway horse.

'They've been asking for this for a long time, David, and I'm hopping mad. You're no better than the rag-picker's son, De Macey. I only wish the Headmaster would throw you both out of the school.'

Gilbert sneered at him.

'Perhaps you'd like to have a try,' he suggested.

This was too much for the irate Tony. He eluded David's restraining grasp and, grabbing a cushion off a nearby chair, attacked Roye furiously. Richard caught hold of him from behind and pinned the kicking, wriggling fury down on a table. David could remain passive no longer. He went to his aid and pulled De Macey off him. Richard pushed him away.

'Take your filthy paws off me, Madison,' he shouted indignantly. 'I want nothing to do with the likes of you.'

'Break it up, you fellows, before you wreck the place,' Thornley commanded in his placid fashion, seeing that the time had come for him to intervene and prevent further disorder.

'It was your duty as Captain to stop them from attacking us,' Richard accused hotly.

'That's right, Richard,' Gilbert agreed, backing him up. 'He shouldn't be taking sides. We know he doesn't like us.'

Thornley remained as placid as ever.

'You can think what you like. I won't lose any sleep over it. You were both asking for trouble and you got it. You should be ashamed of yourselves. David has more right to be here than any of us.' There were cries of 'Yes!' and 'Hear! Hear!' from David's friends which drowned the few sarcastic denials from his enemies. 'If you've got a spark of decency left, you'll apologize.'

Richard sneered at him.

'That day will never come, Thornley.'

'We're sick of Madison and of hearing how good he is.' Roye was unable to hide his hatred for David. 'He may fool you and old Ledwidge, but he doesn't fool us. He's only a ...'

Thornley gave him a menacing warning before he could finish what he was about to say.

'Don't say anything you'll be sorry for, Roye. David has too many friends in Abbot's, and I don't intend to waste any of my time seeing to it that you don't get hurt. You're not worth it.'

'It's no use staying here, Gilbert,' Richard said. 'They're all against us.'

'It's your own doing, De Macey. Don't blame us.'

Richard and Gilbert left the room in a great huff and were followed by their friends. Once or twice the two leaders glanced darkly back at David, their envenomed looks engraving themselves on his memory. The whole cruel incident had shattered him. Thornley, realizing how he was feeling, put a comforting hand on his shoulder. 'Don't mind them, David. They're only a pair of unbearable prigs. St Donat's would be a much better place without them.'

'It's all right, Thornley,' replied David, trying hard to conceal his gloom.

'You mustn't feel bad about it. Since they've come here we've only tolerated them, and Tony was speaking for all of us.'

Tony was still quivering after his impetuous onslaught, which had left him exhausted, but unhurt and triumphant.

'You must admit that I was in great fettle, Thornley. But you should have let me finish them off. There were only two of them.' His listeners laughed. 'That's better. You were all becoming much too serious. I bet De Macey and Roye have gone up to the dormitory to lick their wounds.'

The Captain winked at the others.

'You've got a wonderful tongue, Tony. How do you manage to think of the things you say?'

'It's easy – once you know how,' Tony replied modestly. 'And with my spirit you have the cheek to put me out on the wing!'

'Thornley knows what he's doing,' David said with a smile. 'I never knew you were such a ball of fire, and I can understand now why Thornley changed you.'

At that moment Arthur came in. He had such a preoccupied expression on his face that Tony immediately remarked on it.

'What's wrong, Arthur? You look as if you're going to a funeral.'

Arthur managed a weak smile.

'Mr Ledwidge is leaving,' he announced gravely.

There was a stunned silence at such awful news before David was first to find his tongue.

'He can't be. He was in here earlier on and gave us our exercise books back as usual.'

Tony forced a hopeful smile.

'You're only joking, Arthur. If he were leaving, we'd have heard about it before this.'

'Tell us another one of your tall yarns,' Thornley said, laughing. 'We don't believe this one.'

'I'm quite serious. He's going on sick leave. My father told me at teatime. He said that he's being admitted into a London nursing home.'

'But why should he act as if everything was all right?' David asked in anguish. 'He did get a bit weak in the classroom about a month ago, but he got over it just as quickly.'

'That's what you'd expect from him, David. He makes no fuss when he's here and none when he's leaving.'

Thornley nodded in agreement.

'Arthur's right there. They don't make many like Mr Ledwidge nowadays.'

'He carried on as long as he could. According to my father, he should have gone away for a medical check-up a long time ago, but he refused.'

The boys were quieter now. They realized that this was no leg-pull on Arthur's part, and it was a very serious piece of news.

'How long will he be away?' asked Tony. 'Did your father say?'

'He doesn't know. He has to have a lot of investigations done, and that'll take some time.'

'We'll all miss him terribly,' said David morosely. 'I hope he'll be back soon. There couldn't be much wrong with him, could there, Arthur?'

'It's hard to say, David.'

'Did you hear who's taking his place?' Thornley inquired.

'No. No one has been appointed yet.'

'Well, one thing is certain – no one will ever be able to fill his shoes.'

'You're right there, Thornley,' David agreed thoughtfully. 'There's only one Mr Ledwidge.'

7

The New Master Arrives

David suffered in many petty and cruel ways through the knowledge of his background which De Macey, Roye and their satellites now possessed. Cutting, catty remarks were frequently expressed behind his back, and Richard and Gilbert always referred to him sneeringly as 'the scholarship boy'. Neither of them had forgotten the scuffle in the Common Room, and he sensed that they were plotting together to get their revenge.

Like the rest of the boys of Abbot's, he spent a wretched weekend when Mr Ledwidge left for the nursing home. They had all been hoping that Arthur had somehow misquoted his father, but this wasn't the case, and the old man was gone. On Sunday, hundreds of prayers were said in church for his speedy recovery and return to duty, and fervent pleas stormed Heaven for a worthy replacement. Breakfast on Monday morning was a tasteless meal. When it was over, Thornley gave his friends an ominous account of his meeting with the new master.

'I'm sorry to bring such bad news, chaps,' he said, after seeing the new master, a Mr Coleman, for the first time. 'Still, I could be wrong. I've made mistakes before.'

'Don't try to raise any false hopes, Thornley,' Arthur begged, gravely polishing his glasses. 'It won't make things any better. What did Coleman say to you?'

'Not much. When I told him who I was, he inspected me from head to foot as if I were a piece of dirt and dismissed me almost immediately.'

'What became of your speech of welcome?' Tony asked.

Thornley grunted expressively.

'I was hardly in the room when he told me to get out. The words would have stuck in my throat anyway. I just couldn't take to him.'

'First impressions aren't always right,' Arthur observed sagely.

'I hope not. But the least he could have done was to ask how things were run here. He didn't even say anything about Mr Ledwidge.'

'I hear he's got loads of degrees. The Doctor told my father that St Donat's was lucky to get him.'

'His qualifications aren't worrying us, Arthur,' Tony said. 'Coleman himself seems to be the snag. David and I saw him when he arrived in a taxi. He had three big trunks with him, so he must be as vain as a peacock. He didn't even glance at us, although we had doffed our caps like little gentlemen. Didn't we, David?'

'That's right, Tony. I think Thornley has hit the nail on the head.'

'The taxi driver didn't like him either. You all know him, the jolly, red-faced one with the bushy eyebrows. I bet he drinks gallons of whisky. When he was lugging in the trunks, he was swearing like a trooper.'

David added: 'Coleman and he were arguing about something. Tony thought that they'd come to blows.'

'I wanted to stay and watch developments, but David, the old spoilsport, dragged me away.'

'Well,' said Thornley with a sigh, 'we'll probably find out where we stand soon enough.'

With uncertainty and foreboding, they took their seats in the classroom, where De Macey, Roye and a number of others were already awaiting the arrival of the new master.

'De Macey!' said Thornley when he saw the boy in question.

Richard looked up from the book which he and Gilbert were poring over.

'Yes?'

'I see you've crossed your name off the list for the practice game tomorrow? You're fit to play, aren't you?'

'I don't want to, that's all.'

'Insufferable as you are, you're a good forward. But you need practice like the rest of us. I'll put you down again. Is that all right?'

'No, it's not all right. I'm not playing, and that's all about it.'

'Unless you've got a better excuse you'll turn out, or I won't put you in the school team, no matter how good you are. It wouldn't be fair to the others who do their best to get on it.'

Richard was indignant at this bald ultimatum.

'You can't put me off the team. I'm worth my place on it.'

'Then what's your real reason?'

'That's none of your business. If I say that I don't want to play that should be good enough for you.'

'Richard doesn't want to mark Madison, and I don't blame him,' Roye disclosed, sneering.

'Shut up, Gilbert,' Richard told him quickly, frowning with annoyance.

'Is that true, De Macey?' Thornley demanded, eyeing him through narrowed lids.

'And what if it is? Why should I mark him? You know I don't like him.'

'You understand why well enough. On opposite sides, tomorrow, you play in opposing positions. You'll both get invaluable experience playing against each other.'

'I can play in other positions just as well.'

Tony Masefield laughed sarcastically.

'Listen to his boasts! Anyone would think that the team was there for his benefit only. I'd drop him if I were you, Thornley. You can't expect a good team spirit if he's allowed to do as he pleases.'

'I wouldn't like to, but I'm not going to jeopardize our chances of winning the Cup this year on account of one player behaving like a prima donna. Will I put you down now?'

'I suppose so,' Richard replied sourly. 'You're not going to cheat me out of my place, if I can help it.'

The new master, gown flying in his wake, swept into the room, and there was immediate silence. He was a meticulously dressed young man, with a vain, pitiless expression on his lean face, and quick eyes that seemed to miss nothing as they darted interrogatively about. The boys came hastily to their feet and watched him warily as he began to pace up and down very deliberately.

'Sit down, sit down!' he snapped, regarding them mockingly. 'I'm sure you all realize by now who I am. I feel sure that your Captain has already given you a full account of his meeting with me. Isn't that so, Thornley?'

'I told them that I'd seen you, sir,' answered Thornley uncomfortably.

Mr Coleman grunted cynically.

'You put it very diplomatically. Well, we may as well get to know our respective positions from the start. When I arrived here yesterday, I noticed that there were some boys who seemed to have nothing better to do than loiter about the place and watch me alighting from the taxi as if I were a performer in a circus.' Tony nudged David at this reference to themselves. 'Such a breach of good manners won't be permitted to occur in future. I discovered in my room a barely decipherable copy of the school's rules and regulations. I'll have a new edition put in the Common Room of Abbot's House so that you can study them carefully. Rules, in spite of a more popular understanding to the contrary, are made to be observed, and you'll no longer be able to plead ignorance of them. I want discipline, and I intend to have it. Is that clear?' The boys nodded dumbly. 'You'll soon discover that you're no longer dealing with a doddering old man. I expect co-operation from all of you, and there's no reason why our association with one another should not be a harmonious one. As Captain of Lower School, Thornley, I expect your co-operation particularly.'

'Yes, sir.' It was an unenthusiastic response.

'I saw your list for a practice match tomorrow.'

'This will be the first, sir,' Thornley explained. 'The weather has been too stormy up to now.'

'I'd like to have the names of the players and reserves who'll be representing the school this year.'

'Yes, sir. I'll give you the list after lunch. Will you be refereeing the game tomorrow, sir?'

'There won't be a game. Some running to strengthen your legs and wind will be much more suitable after a long summer holiday of idleness.'

'But, sir, we do our fair share of that as well, and it's not so dependent on the weather. We need as many practice games as we can get.'

'I'll decide what's best for the team, Thornley,' Coleman replied tartly. 'Most of you younger boys become as helpless as old men when your legs and lungs give out in the second half.'

'But, sir …'

'I don't propose to argue about it. You can consider the matter closed.' His quick eyes spotted David whispering to Tony and he stopped abruptly pacing up and down. 'What's your name, boy?'

David stood up.

'Madison, sir. David Madison.'

'Are you the boy who's here on scholarship?'

'Yes.' The reference cut like a knife, but worse was yet to come.

'"Sir", when you address me. Have you no manners?'

'Yes, sir.'

The master recommenced pacing the floor.

'What is this school coming to? When I accepted this post I didn't realise that I'd have to waste my talents on a free pupil.' De Macey, Roye and their cronies laughed and he smiled at them. 'I didn't spend years in a university for that.'

Arthur Gillespie, deciding that no amount of pedagogical licence could excuse such a display of callousness, observed in a hoarse whisper that was audible to the whole class: 'What he needs is a double dose of castor oil.' Most of the boys tittered, delighted that he had expressed so succinctly the decent opinion of the overwhelming majority of the class.

With a bright flush on his cheek, Coleman pointed a finger at him.

'Stand up, boy,' he cried angrily. 'Your name?'

'Arthur Gillespie, sir,' answered Arthur inoffensively.

'Where are you from?'

'From around here, sir. I'm a day boy.' With great adroitness, he subtly suggested the danger of unduly interfering with one who lived within a short distance of the school, and Coleman understood. Swallowing his anger, he addressed him in a more subdued tone.

'Don't speak out of turn again, Gillespie. You may sit down.' He returned to safer territory. 'As for you, Madison, I won't tolerate any troublemakers in this class. Is that understood?'

'Yes, sir.'

'You'd better sit in front where I can keep an eye on you,' he added roughly, making up for lost ground in his brief encounter with Arthur.

David gathered up his books and, leaving safe harbourage at the back of the room, sought a new place in a desk facing the master's table. His progress irritated Coleman who caught him by the arm and almost threw him into the seat. This unwarranted action elicited another hoarse whisper from the back row.

'Castor oil, that's the only treatment.'

When class ended and Coleman had left the room, the boys discussed the situation.

'The insolent beggar!' Tony exclaimed hotly. 'I'd love to wipe that smirk off his face.'

'He doesn't seem to like me very much,' said David morosely.

'He was only trying to be funny, David.' It was a rather unconvincing reply which was meant to soften David's foreboding. 'He thought he was making a big impression when he heard Roye and the other hyenas laughing. It's too soon to judge what he's really like. In any case, Mr Ledwidge may be back soon.' Again, this was said with very little conviction in his voice,

'I hope you're right, Tony.'

'Mr Coleman knows how to deal with Madison, eh, Richard?' Gilbert jeered, guffawing loudly.

'He certainly put him in his place quickly enough. He wasn't long making short work of Thornley's plans either.'

Thornley glowered at him.

'If I have anything to do with it, there'll be a game tomorrow. He's not going to ruin our chances of winning the Cup with any of his crackpot ideas.'

'You won't have much say in the matter. He's not the sort who changes his mind once it's made up. You'll jump through the hoop when he cracks his whip.'

'He may get his runs out of us, but I'll arrange practice games in spite of him. I suppose he'd make us play rugger if we were training for track events.'

'We're with you, Thornley,' David promised. 'You know what the team needs more than anyone.'

'You speak for yourself, Madison,' Richard said curtly.

Tony Masefield turned on him angrily.

'Shut up, De Macey. Did you hear what he called Mr Ledwidge? A doddering old man! Such impertinence!'

'I wasn't far wrong about him,' the Captain reminded them. 'He suspected what I had told you about him, too.'

David nodded.

'He doesn't miss much. He spotted me and Tony when he was arriving. I didn't think he noticed us.'

'I was afraid he was going to attack us about it, David. He must have forgotten.'

'You're a cool one, Arthur,' Thornley commented with a chuckle. 'If I don't miss my guess, he'll give you a wide berth in future.'

'I was only enhancing my immunity, that's all.'

'I wish I'd worked harder at my books,' groaned Tony,

conscious of time wasted in the past. 'Ignorance won't pay off with a tyke like him.' He looked enviously at David. 'You've nothing to worry about there, David. You're fool-proof in class. Mr Ledwidge always said so.'

'Old Ledwidge isn't here any longer, Masefield,' Richard De Macey sneered. 'Just let's wait and see what happens with Mr Coleman.'

8

Coleman Institutes a Reign of Terror

Never in the long history of St Donat's was a master so hated, despised and feared as Coleman. Except for a chosen few – among whom De Macey and Roye figured prominently – all the boys suffered in one way or another. A reign of terror began in Lower School, and that happy atmosphere for which it was renowned, in spite of the presence of the despised elect and their associates, suffered a partial eclipse. David was singled out for special attention and treatment. Disturbances in class were generally attributed to him, and he was soon to discover that, contrary to Tony's – and Mr Ledwidge's – high opinion of his scholastic ability, he was seldom right where the new master was concerned. Moreover, physical punishment was reserved almost exclusively for him, and as the days lengthened into weeks, canings and cuffings gradually increased in severity. He began to dread his classes but prayed that he could continue to put up a brave front.

One afternoon, when he was returning alone from Arthur's house where he had had lunch, he was so preoccupied with thinking about the crop of tribulations which the change in teachers was causing him that he failed to see the danger that lay ahead. De Macey, Roye, and about three others of their set, pretending to be unaware that he was behind them, were meandering slowly along the road waiting for him to come abreast.

'Here comes the scholarship boy,' Roye exclaimed loudly as soon as their quarry was near. David tried to pass them, but

Gilbert, encouraged by the knowledge that might was over-whelmingly in his favour, blocked his path aggressively. 'Afraid to stand your ground, eh?' he taunted. 'Will I give him the coward's blow, Richard?' Richard nodded loftily, and he raised his hand to strike, but before it reached its mark on David's neck a powerful thrust by David countered it, and with a frightened yelp he fell back.

Richard, who was a strong boy, pulled David's arm behind his back and, incited by the others to give him the 'Chinese torture', began to twist it. However, for all his faults, Richard was neither vicious nor sadistic and relaxed his grip whenever he heard his captive's sharp intakes of breath. Roye then took over. He twisted the prisoner's arm until it hurt, and, although David bit his lip, he could not suppress a cry of pain. Struggling hard, he slipped on the macadamized surface of the road and fell on his back. One of the boys smeared his face with soil from the adjacent ditch while a second sent his cap flying into a nearby field. Roye began to twist his arm again but Richard caught him by the sleeve.

'Let him go, Gilbert – you're hurting him too much. He's had enough anyway.'

Gilbert obeyed reluctantly and the boys moved off, jeering over their shoulders. Picking himself up from the road, David dusted himself. He retrieved his cap and continued on his way to the Abbey. Tony was in the study when he got there, busily making a weird translation of a Latin unseen. He inspected him in amazement.

'What on earth has happened to you, David? Did one of Arthur's crazy experiments explode?'

'No, Tony. I was ambushed by De Macey and his gang.'

The information electrified his listener, who jumped to his feet and made for the door.

'We'll collect some of the chaps and give them a taste of their own medicine,' he hissed grimly through clenched teeth. 'We'll show 'em they can't get away with a despicable thing like that.'

'It's no use, Tony. If Coleman caught us, we'd have more lines to do than we could cope with.'

'Hang Coleman and his lines! It'll be worth it.'

It required patience and tact on David's part to mollify him, but at length he succeeded. They gave the soiled suit a vigorous clean, Tony supervising the operation and frequently regaling himself and David with sweets and chocolates. He had a sweet tooth and his parents kept him well supplied.

The following morning Coleman hauled David out in front of the class.

'What have you been up to, you little tramp?' he demanded harshly, pointing at some stains on his jacket which the most diligent brushing had failed to remove.

'I fell on the road yesterday, sir.'

'You little liar! You've probably been up to some mischief. How dare you appear in my class in such a dirty suit! I suppose you're too proud a beggar to admit that it's the only one you've got.' David blushed and bit his lip. Although it was untrue, he wouldn't beg any quarter by denying it. Roye and his friends guffawed loudly. Richard, to give him his due, did so a bit hollowly: for his better feelings told him that this was a completely heartless and inexcusable thing to say. Tony Masefield took a pin out of the lapel of his jacket and embedded it in Roye's flabby buttock. Gilbert yelled with pain. 'What's going on back there?'

Arthur Gillespie stood up.

'Roye sat on a splinter, sir,' he announced solemnly before a complaint could be lodged by the injured party. Gilbert was about to launch into a voluble protest when Richard, who was smiling to himself, pulled him back into his seat. David smiled at his two friends.

'Wipe that smile off your face, Madison,' Coleman cried angrily. 'You can stand at the wall until the bell goes.'

David was used to this form of punishment by now. The

ignominious feature about it was that, facing the class, he could see De Macey and his clique enjoying his plight and passing cruel remarks about him – and that was what really hurt.

9

The Spring Term Opens Inauspiciously

The Christmas holidays came as a welcome relief to the boys of Abbot's. In the short time that he had been with them, Coleman had more than made his presence felt and it was their wish that, after the vacation, Mr Ledwidge would be back in harness again. It was a vain wish, for they returned to the school, which was now looking like a picture with snow on the roof and cloister, to find their *bête noire* as omnipresent as ever. With heavy heart, David left Liverpool for Abbotmead, having spent a glorious Christmastide in the bosom of his family, who knew nothing of his troubles. Seeing Tony again after his brief respite from persecution did much to console him. When their greetings were over, they did their unpacking and then had a game of draughts in the Common Room.

Tony got up to poke the fire during the final stages of the game. 'That's better!' he exclaimed with satisfaction when he had revived the dying coals. He peeped up the ample, medieval chimney. 'They knew how to build fireplaces in the old days. I hope you're not cheating when my back's turned, David?'

'There's no need to, Tony. Another move or so and I've got you licked. It's useless for you to continue.'

'Then we'll play another game. I may be lucky this time.'

David began arranging the pieces on the board. 'All right! If you're willing to suffer another defeat, I'm willing to oblige.'

'You cheeky blighter!' Tony replied, laughing. He inspected a framed set of the school's rules and regulations which was prominently displayed near the fireplace. 'For two pins I'd chuck Coleman's penal laws into the fire. It's almost a sacrilege to have them in this room.'

'It would be a sacrilege if you interfered with them,' David answered, smiling at his friend's sudden show of aggressiveness. 'He'd spot it immediately.'

'You're right – he never misses a beat.' He put the poker down and wandered over to the window. He opened it and, craning his neck, looked out. 'The snow's almost a foot high outside.' He went over to the table where David was, and he sat down with one leg doubled up under him on the chair and watched his friend make his move.

'Your move, Tony.'

Tony considered the possibilities thoughtfully.

'I wish it was Christmas again,' he said, toying with one of the draughts.

'Why? Did you have a good time?'

'Terrific! It was the best one I ever had.'

'Do you still believe in Santa Claus?' asked David, laughing.

'Of course not, but each year it's becoming more difficult to decide whether or not I should tell them that at home. I'm not sure how they'd react. If I said I didn't, they might consider me grown-up and give me something useful as a present. But I can get that from them anytime of the year, so at present I'm playing safe and letting them think I do.' His clever psychology amused them and they laughed merrily.

Arthur joined them. He was looking so preoccupied that they guessed he had something weighing on his mind.

'Guess who's back?'

'Mr Ledwidge, Arthur?' Tony asked hopefully.

'No, worse luck, and my father says that he may never be back. He's had some kind of operation and his progress is very unsatisfactory. The surgeon's very worried about him.'

'I hope nothing happens to him,' David said solicitously. 'He's a grand old man. I hope he doesn't …'

'Don't say it, David,' begged Tony. 'Who's back, Arthur?'

'Belford.'

'Of all the misfortunes! First, Coleman, now, Belford! I was sure he'd gone for good when he failed to show up last term.'

'Who's Belford?' David inquired with interest.

'Another of the De Macey and Roye crowd, David, and an awful bully. He'll be sleeping in that vacant bed opposite mine in the dormitory. We'll have to look out for further squalls from now on.'

'Tony stood up to him once,' Arthur said proudly. 'But he's too big for us and too old. He's been in the same class for over two years.'

'I'll stand up to him again if necessary. I'm not afraid of him or any of the bunch.'

'He's big even for his age, David.' Arthur peered knowledge-ably over the rims of his glasses. 'There must be something wrong with his glands.'

Tony suggested that they should go and build a snowman in Cloister Court. They muffled themselves up well against the biting cold and were soon busily engaged in the work, cheerfully dodging stray and intended snowballs which were thrown by boys in other groups about them. David stood out as a picture of good health. His cheeks, whipped to a rosy glow by the icy air, set off his fine blue eyes and dark hair, and he looked radiant in the rays of the sinking sun. Tony threw himself body and soul into the task while Arthur directed the operation. When it was finished, they had as plump a snowman as any of the boys had ever seen and they stood back to admire their handiwork.

'When can we knock it down, Tony?' a boy shouted over, pausing in the manufacture of fresh snowballs.

'I'll let you know,' Tony informed him as the other resumed his work.

De Macey and Roye, who had been standing outside Abbot's watching them, came trudging through the snow towards them. With them was a strange boy David hadn't seen before. He was awkwardly and heavily built, and in height he was a head and shoulders over his friends. His manner was loud and rough, and David concluded that this must be Belford, the pupil of ill-repute whom he had heard about.

'I'll knock it down for you now, Masefield,' he declared loudly.

'You'd better not,' Tony cried hotly, his eyes emitting sparks of fire.

'I bet you're glad I'm back. You must have missed me a lot.' He gave a loud guffaw and knocked a piece off the snowman's head.

Tony pushed him away angrily.

'You keep your hands to yourself, Belford.'

'If you don't show a bit more respect, Masefield,' jeered Roye tauntingly, 'he'll give you what he gave you last time.'

'How did you like it?' asked Belford. 'This time you'll have to be treated by the school quack – a dig at Arthur's father – if you're not careful.' Belford was enjoying himself and the success which his shallow wit was having with his friends was going to his head like wine.

'It's a pity you were ever allowed back into St Donat's, you hulking brute! I was almost certain that you'd been expelled by the Doctor and were now in a reformatory.'

Attracted by Tony's shrill voice, boys came running from the four corners of Cloister Court and gathered round. They knew that before long somebody's blood was bound to be spilled – hopefully, not theirs.

Belford was furious, and his face turned an ashen grey with anger. He approached the snowman again, but before he could do any more damage, Tony attacked him. Although he had taken a beating at the bully's hands once before, Tony intended to defend their snowy handiwork from premature demolition while there was a breath left in him. He began to grapple with his oversize antagonist. Belford shook him off and threw him heavily to the ground, where he lay winded. Roye, and other boys of his clique who had now joined him, jeered at his impotence while his two friends helped him up.

'Why don't you pick on someone your own size, you big bully!' cried David, and there were angry mutters of agreement from most of the onlookers.

'You mind your own business or you'll be next,' Belford warned viciously. Roye whispered in his ear. 'So *you're* the free pupil! How would you like a dose of the same medicine, Madison?' He caught David by the scarf and pulled him towards him.

David brought his joined hands down on the other's arms with all his might and broke his grip. Cursing, Belford made a lunge at him. David hit him on the chest with right and left fists. When the other's defence lowered, he aimed for the head and the knuckles of his right hand bounced smartly off Belford's forehead. Advice and counter-advice, cheers and boos, issued thick and fast from the spectators as the fight became even more physical and desperate. The long-reaching fist of the bully caught David full in the face and he fell back dazed against the snowman, blood trickling from a cut at the corner of his mouth. Following up his advantage, Belford kicked at him but missed. David took the initiative next and sailed into his opponent with fists and arms flying. Belford licked his lips. Like most bullies, he hadn't anticipated anything like this. He joined again in battle, butting, stamping, hitting low and using any method that would help him win. David, however, was well knit and, though his thrusts and punches were not as powerful as the bigger boy's, they rained more often until, finally, a well-delivered left smashed into Belford's mouth and the bully reeled round and fell on the well-trodden snow. Panting heavily, David waited for him to get up, but Belford had had enough of single combat.

'Help me get him,' he snarled to his supporters, spitting blood on the snow.

Richard De Macey looked at him with ill-concealed contempt.

'Madison beat you fair and square, Belford, so leave him alone.'

There was a rousing cheer for David.

'I'm glad to see that you've got a bit more decency and a better sense of fair play than your friends, De Macey,' observed Thornley, who had just joined the ring of spectators. Richard pretended that he hadn't heard what he had said and looked away. 'Well done, David! That needed doing for a long time.'

'Look out, boys, Coleman's coming!' a voice somewhere in the crowd warned.

But before they could disperse, the master was on top of them, and the crowd quickly made a passage for him.

'Have you been fighting, Madison?' Coleman demanded sternly.

'Yes, sir,' replied David unhappily, dabbing the corner of his mouth, which was still bleeding, with his handkerchief.

'You're a disgrace to the school. Go to my room immediately. I'll deal with you later.'

David began to walk dejectedly towards Abbot's, acknowledging with wan little smiles the whispered condolences of his friends.

'It wasn't his fault, sir,' Thornley declared in protest. 'He didn't start it.'

'When I want your comments, Thornley, I'll ask for them. I'll deal with this in my own way.'

'Mr Ledwidge would have let us settle this among ourselves.'

Coleman turned on him furiously, his colour heightening with anger.

'I don't wish to hear any further insubordinate remarks from you. You're not fit to be Captain of Lower School. Since I've come here you've repeatedly refused to co-operate with me. I'll do my best to see that the next Captain will be one I can depend on.'

'You can accept my resignation now if you like,' Thornley retorted rebelliously. 'You never listen to anything I say.'

'Be silent, you impertinent wretch,' Coleman shouted. 'I'll decide when you'll resign. I don't want to have to pull you up for talk of this kind again. Is that understood?'

The Captain glowered silently. Most of the other boys had closed ranks behind him when he had taken his fine, manly stand against the tyrant, and they were now feeling just as rebellious as he was. After giving them a look of bitter displeasure, the master followed his victim across Cloister Court. Tony gathered up a snowball but, just as he was about to fire it at his retreating back, Thornley stopped him.

'Why didn't you let me throw it? It's the least I could do for David.'

'It would do no good, Tony. It would only make it tougher on him. Coleman would vent his anger on him.'

'He hardly lets David breathe,' Arthur said gloomily.

Gilbert Roye sneered in his usual callous and provocative way. 'I hope Mr Coleman gives him a good thrashing.'

'Shut your mouth, Roye, or one of us will shut it for you,' Thornley warned with quiet menace in his voice. 'We're all fed up with you and your cowardly set. This wouldn't have happened but for Belford. He's no sooner back than he begins to cause trouble. He should have learned a lesson today that will keep him quiet for a while.'

Roye took counsel with his associates and they sauntered off, evidently deciding that discretion was the better part of valour.

When, later, Tony heard from David about the severe caning that Coleman had given him, he was more anxious than ever to make him pay for his tyranny. After the evening meal, when he and his friends were coming out of Abbot's House, he saw the master taking the night air and an idea struck him.

'I've got a plan to get our revenge on Coleman for what he did to David,' he told them excitedly.

'What is it, Tony?' asked Thornley suspiciously, hoping that it wouldn't be quite so overt in nature as the contemplated snow-balling had been.

'Look over there. The brute's standing right under the clock tower. If I were to climb up there and push that big drift of snow off that stone ledge below the clock it'd be bound to fall on him.'

He was quivering with excitement, and the veins in his neck were standing out in relief, as they usually did when he was in such a state.

Although most of the others buzzed their approval, he got no encouragement from David.

'It'd be too risky, Tony. With the place in such a dangerous condition in this weather, you could be killed. You slipped on one of the steps once before, remember, and could have been seriously hurt. I won't let you do it.'

'That was last year, David. I'm more experienced now. I'll be careful. I promise.'

'Then I'm going with you.'

'I'm going alone. You're not used to the place and could be more of a hindrance than a help.'

'You could do it after more preparation.'

'You're not clever enough for me, David,' Tony replied with a knowing laugh. 'The snow will be gone soon. It's beginning to melt already. And apart from that, Coleman won't stand there for ever just to suit us.' He looked at his watch. 'I'll just about make it before the clock chimes the hour. Be sure to act like nothing's happened after he's blitzed, in case he smells a rat. I'll be back in a few minutes. Cheerio!'

Footsteps muffled by the snow, he went racing across Cloister Court. Passing the chapel, he ran under the arch which connected the clock tower with the main bulk of the school buildings, and then wriggled through an unshuttered window. He flew up the steps, peeped out a lancet window below the clock and could just distinguish the dim figure of the master in the gathering murk below.

On the stone ledge in question was a mass of snow which was beginning to thaw and which was studded in places with sharp, dagger-like slivers of ice. He pushed hard against it. The semi-solid snowy mass slid off its base and, with a whoosh, engulfed the unsuspecting Coleman standing below. Not waiting to see the result of his work, he tore back to his friends. They were strolling casually about as he had advised them to, and he quickly mingled among them.

'How did it go, Thornley?' he whispered surreptitiously.

'Right on target, Tony. We'd better get moving, though. He's coming this way like an angry bull.'

Coleman, a figure of furious energy and rage, with a mantle of thawing snow and ice on his head and shoulders, turned back before he had reached them, and, instead, began to search frantically for an entry into the clock tower. Finding it, he went inside to investigate, and reappeared after a short interval with a look of perplexity on his face. He scrutinized the boys for a clue to his misfortune and then strode off impotently.

Tony was overjoyed at the success of the operation, which was to pass into the unwritten history of the school. He was happy, too, that he had given David an indication of the extent of his friendship for him.

10

The Headmaster Calls David to his Study

As the weary weeks dragged by, David discovered that any good resolutions which Coleman might have made for the new year were not for his benefit. He was seldom out of hot water, and, as he showed no signs of retaliation, newer humiliations were heaped upon him. One afternoon, in class, Coleman disclosed the pregnant fact that he had reported him to Dr Princeton.

'The trouble with a boy of your upbringing, Madison, is that you resent authority,' he declared venomously. David looked at him unflinchingly, and he continued in a rising voice: 'You're the most thick-skinned, impertinent and troublesome boy I've ever come across, but I'll break you if it's the last thing I do. I've reported you to the Headmaster, and I've warned him what to expect.'

This was serious, and not even Tony tried to minimize the fact when they discussed it later.

'He's as slimy as a snake, David, and no one can guess what lies he's told the Doctor about you. What will you say to the Doctor when he sees you?'

'I don't know,' replied David, gulping at the awful prospect before him. 'It won't make much difference anyway. The Doctor will believe him, not me.'

When the dreaded summons came, Tony gallantly accompanied him as far as the Headmaster's study. Tony nearly collapsed with shock when the door was opened by Dr Princeton himself, who scrutinized him with those remarkable eyes of his which seemed capable of seeing into one's soul.

'I don't recall having an appointment with you, Masefield. I hope you haven't been getting into any trouble?'

'N-no, sir,' Tony stammered. He turned on his heel and fled down the corridor, but the Headmaster was in too serious a frame of mind to smile at his comical departure.

He closed the door and David stood timidly before him, a chill in his heart and feeling more miserable than he had ever done in his life before.

'What Mr Coleman has told me about you is very disturbing, very disturbing indeed. It appears that you are self-willed and troublesome, in and out of class. I understand that he has been very patient with you and has shown you every consideration.'

'That's not true!' David protested in a sudden outburst.

The Headmaster raised his eyebrows inquiringly.

'Then perhaps you have something to say that may throw some light on this unhappy report?' David bit his lip, but remained silent. He knew that Coleman had so coloured his accusations that any attempt to deny them would be useless. 'Well, Madison, I'm waiting for an answer.'

'No, sir.'

'Very well. In that case, I can accept Mr Coleman's word that what he says is no exaggeration. It hurts me very much to have to mention it in this way, but I am forced to speak plainly. Since you came here on a scholarship you were expected to maintain a reasonable standard in your work and conduct. You were a brilliant pupil when you first started here, but you've gradually gone from bad to worse. Up to the present, I've been very reluctant to prejudice your staying on at the Abbey. That's why I haven't seen you sooner. I was hoping that for the sake of your parents, who naturally pin high hopes on you, as well as your own, that you'd pull yourself together when you knew that you had been reported to me. Have you anything to say now? I am only too willing to listen.'

'No, sir,' replied a dispirited, unhappy David. He was on the verge of tears and prayed that he would soon be allowed to go.

'I see. As you leave me no other alternative, I'll have to bring your conduct and progress to the notice of the school Governors at their next meeting. I must warn you that, under the circumstances, I won't be able to offer any recommendations on your behalf. I'm afraid that you must be prepared for the worst.' The Headmaster shook his head gravely. 'I'm sorry, Madison.'

There the interview ended. David avoided his friends and sought balm for his troubled mind in the school chapel. He had half-decided to write home to his parents to take him away from the Abbey, but when he recalled how the Headmaster had mentioned their high expectations for him he put the idea out of his head and resolved to stick the nightmare out to the bitter end.

11

Sir Frederick Visits his Son

Shortly before the end of the term, Sir Frederick De Macey motored down from Norfolk to visit his son. If he had any hopes of seeing a reformed boy who was at last facing up to life in a more manly way, he was due for a bitter disappointment. While he was walking with him in the school grounds, Tony Masefield and David were coming towards them. Tony smiled at him as they passed by but ignored Richard so obviously that his attitude towards his son wasn't lost on him.

'Are those boys in your class, Richard?' Sir Frederick asked gruffly, trying to reopen a conversation which had flagged and died embarrassingly. 'They look about your age.'

'Yes.'

'Then why didn't they speak to you?'

'Because they're not friends of mine.'

'I see. That was young Masefield who smiled at me, wasn't it?'

'I think so,' was the sullen reply.

'Who was the other boy?'

'Oh, him? He's only a scholarship boy. He comes from Liverpool or Manchester or some place.'

His father did not miss the innuendo in his grudging words.

'Really, Richard, I find your sense of class consciousness very distasteful, and I hope it doesn't develop. You allude to his scholarship as if it was some sort of shame instead of a distinction. I will be blunt with you. So far, most things in your life have come to you through an accident of birth. On your present showing, I know that if positions were reversed, and you had been born in Liverpool, you wouldn't be here on scholarship as he is now. Just think about it. You did say that was young Masefield who was with him, didn't you, or was he just another scholarship boy?'

'It was Masefield,' Richard replied angrily.

'It would be mannerly if you were to address me as you should a father now and again.' Sir Frederick was angry, too. 'Apparently Masefield takes his companions as he finds them, as a boy should. It would be worth your while to emulate him.'

Shocked by his visit, Sir Frederick returned to his home in Norfolk and dispelled any hopes of his son's reformation.

12

Thornley Performs a Christening

A week or two before the Easter break, Tony, his brown eyes dancing in his head with delight, was standing in the middle of the study, snapping new garters which he had bought, to demonstrate their elasticity, while David sat on the table enjoying the exhibition.

'See how it's done, David? No slipping there. They're over an inch wide and they don't mark my legs like the thin ones. I bought some elastic in the village and Charlie's missus sewed them together for me. Like her hubby, she has a soft spot in her heart for us Abbot's boys, and she treated me like a son.'

'You're the life and soul of Abbot's, Tony,' David said, laughing. The look of pleasure that lit up the other's countenance at the compliment made him glad that he had chosen those particular words. 'By the way, had Charlie anything new to say about the Abbot?'

As if struck by a bombshell, Tony stopped snapping his garters. 'Don't mention the Abbot, David,' he pleaded in a less exhilarated tone. 'Charlie considers me past the initiation stage now and made my flesh creep while the missus was hammering a job on the garters. He told mc that some people have sworn that they've seen him and it's always *after Christmas*. I swear that you'll never find me outside the dormitory in my right senses after lights out.'

Although the information was very disquieting, the expression on Tony's face was so funny that David couldn't refrain from laughing.

'It's no laughing matter,' Tony asserted. 'Make a resolution now to stick to your bed like me and you'll never regret it.' Suddenly the absurdity of his situation as he unburdened himself of the eerie tidings struck him, and he joined in the laughter. He bent down and recommenced snapping his garters, but suddenly jerked upright again. 'You haven't asked me yet why I bothered to buy a new pair?'

'Well, why did you?'

'Coleman met me in Cloister Passage this morning and told me that I looked like a tramp.' Tony put on an air of injured dignity. 'Imagine his cheek! He said that my stockings were slovenly and that, if he ever caught me again with them at half-mast, he'd make an example of me – and you know, David, how difficult it is to keep them up when you've just about got the right number of muscles on your legs.'

'You're out on your own, Tony,' David remarked with a delighted laugh. After a short spell at their books, they went down to the Common Room. A group of boys were sitting around the open fire holding an animated discussion. Some important subject was evidently on the agenda, and, one by one, those who were playing games abandoned them to join the company at the fire. With much good-humoured bunting and banter, places were found for David and Tony in the innermost circle. The warmth was very pleasant there, and it gave them a great sense of security to sit among their friends.

'We're trying to find a suitable moniker for Coleman, David,' explained Thornley, who was acting as chairman of the seditious brains trust. Like the others, he realized that David merited a special position of honour among them because he was the most persecuted of them all.

'"Big Ears",' one of the boys suggested.

'That's not a nickname for a tyke like him,' another observed disparagingly. 'It's more like a term of endearment.' A couple of his listeners saw the pun – whether intended or not – and chuckled loudly to show their wit in spotting it.

'What about "Fish Face" or "Gorilla"?'

'They're no good,' piped up a small voice from the rear of the huddled group of rebellious boys. 'I think "Butcher"'s better.'

'That's not bad, young 'un,' Thornley commented appreciatively to this architect of unpleasant pseudonyms, who thereupon withdrew into obscurity for the remainder of the evening, glowing with pride after his few seconds' taste of fame. The names came thick and fast now, for the inventiveness of the boys had sharpened owing to the stiff competition.

'We're getting warmer, but we still haven't found anything strong enough,' the Captain said at length. 'We want something that will show our disgust and loathing of the man. Nothing too human, if you know what I mean.'

'He's not a man,' cried one of the iconoclasts with heavy sarcasm, and other voices mingled in agreement.

Tony Masefield, who had wriggled into a position almost on top of the fire – a manoeuvre admirably suited to his lithe body – where he was squatting on the floor with his stockings at his ankles, spoke:

'You've hit the nail on the head there,' he commented bitterly. 'He hasn't a scrap of human decency in him. He's only ...' He was thinking deeply, but the name which seemed to be on the tip of his tongue was eluding him.

'Give him room, boys,' chirped a listener merrily, 'and Tony will think of something.'

'You can do it, Tony,' Thornley encouraged confidently.

'I'm not so sure about that, Thornley. Coleman's only a beast.'

'I knew he'd do it,' cried his original sponsor with admiration, tickled pink that he had bet on a winner.

Tony was puzzled by the sudden acclamation.

'I ...' he began in explanation, but before he could say anything more the Captain slapped him vigorously on the back.

'That's it, Tony. Henceforth, he's christened "the Beast". How on earth did you think of it?'

Although he had only meant it as a chance remark, Tony saw

no reason why he shouldn't take unqualified credit for authoring the fitting nickname. Indeed, it had often been used by the boys in the past when referring to Coleman, but never as a standard title.

'It's easy, once you have the knack,' he admitted modestly. It was glorious to bask in the sunshine of their admiration. However, his glory was short-lived, for the master had entered the room without being noticed, and his voice brought the alarmed gathering to its feet.

'Have you little idlers nothing better to do than lounge in front of a fire on a bracing evening like this?' he demanded caustically. 'Have you no marrow in your bones?' He strutted about, relishing their discomfiture. One by one, the boys sidled out of the room, and David and Tony also edged their way towards the door.

'Masefield.'

Tony spun round in alarm. He was afraid that the master might have overheard his descriptive and highly unflattering name for him.

'Yes, sir?' he asked anxiously, fearing the worst.

'What did I tell you about your stockings?'

Tony breathed a sigh of relief.

'I bought new garters, sir.'

'Then why don't you use them?' Tony quickly pulled up his stockings over legs that were smarting with rubefaction from the fire. 'In case you forget what garters are for in future, I suggest you write out fifty times: "Garters are made of elastic so that I can suspend my stockings." Leave the lines on my table by nine o'clock tomorrow morning. Is that clear?'

'Yes, sir,' replied the unfortunate Tony, stifling a groan.

'And no scribbling or you'll repeat them. Any other boy who is not neat and tidy at all times will be similarly punished.' He surveyed the glowering boys who were still in the room and then went out.

'Did you ever hear such a piece of tripe?' Tony exclaimed

bitterly when the master was well out of earshot. He repeated the text of his lines in an aping manner. His listeners would have laughed at the way he said it were it really a subject for fun; but fifty lines are fifty lines and no joke, as every schoolboy knows.

'What's wrong, David?' inquired Thornley, noticing that he had become very preoccupied and gloomy since Tony had been penalized.

'It would be safer if all of you kept me at a distance in future' was the slow answer.

'What do you mean?' Tony asked incredulously.

'Well, Coleman seizes every opportunity to punish the lot of you because of me.'

'The Beast knows who your friends are, David – and your enemies,' the Captain said. 'The De Macey gang is probably the best gallery he's ever had for his cheap wit, and they play on this to curry favour with him. But he doesn't get any encouragement or false adoration from us.'

'I know, but I'm only a millstone round your necks.'

'You must be going off your rocker to suggest such a thing,' exclaimed Tony, very displeased that he should try to measure their friendship for him – and his, in particular – in terms of safety; but he continued in a lighter vein: 'It's such a pity, too. You were always the sanest of us.'

'We don't want to hear such nonsense again, David,' said Thornley. 'Do we, Tony?'

'The matter's closed as far as I'm concerned, Thornley.'

'What kind of friends do you think we'd be if we didn't stick with you to the bitter end?'

This firm affirmation of continued support cheered David up. He never again brought the subject up. As Tony had said, the matter was closed.

13

Richard's Reformation Begins

The Easter holidays came and David left for his home in Liverpool. He was so happy there that he dreaded returning to school because of all the misery which it now held for him. No longer did the beautiful old abbey hold any appeal. No longer did he take pleasure in simply rambling about the buildings and grounds, drinking in peace and security; for these had vanished with Mr Ledwidge's departure, and in their place a sense of apprehension and impending doom had taken strong root. As persecution increased, St Donat's had become more and more like a huge prison with Coleman the brutal jailer. As each new cloud gathered on the horizon, he prayed that it would be the last; but it seemed that the sky would never become blue again, so continuously did misfortunes follow on each other's heels.

With the arrival of the finer weather, off came mufflers and gloves, out came the rollers and mowers, up went the practice nets, and the school's sporting activities were soon in full swing. To open the cricket season, the boys of Abbot's, according to their usual custom, arranged a game among themselves for the purpose of selecting the team that would represent them in outside matches with other schools. With the sweet smell of freshly cut grass in their nostrils, they trotted gaily onto the smooth, green turf, eager for the game; and, when the stumps and bails were placed in position, they congregated in a clamorous mass around Thornley who was making the draw. All the players were in whites, and some were wearing their red caps and red blazers, lending still more colour to the scene. David, with shirtsleeves rolled up, and with the beginning of an early tan on his face, strolled over to join them.

'Whose team am I on, Thornley?' he asked, eager to show his prowess with the bat.

'You're with De Macey, David. He's short a player.'

'I don't want Madison,' Richard growled, turning his back on the late arrival. Since his father's visit before the Easter break – when he had been lectured about the accident of birth and position and the necessity of taking his fellow pupils as he found them, irrespective of these – his ill feeling and animosity towards David, instead of diminishing, had tended to increase.

Uncertain what to do, David waited uncomfortably for Thornley's directions. Thornley, not wishing to make an issue out of the matter just then by insisting on De Macey accepting him, exchanged one of his own men for him. This satisfied Richard, who smiled to himself at getting his own way.

Thornley's side won the toss and went into bat first. When David took his turn before the wicket he had a creditable innings. He had played a lot of cricket before, but never in such ideal surroundings and seldom on such a true pitch. He batted well and made some quite brilliant strokes, and when the click of the ball against the stumps told him that he had been clean-bowled he was satisfied with his score. Thornley congratulated him on his performance and told him that he was a certainty for the school eleven. When De Macey's team began its innings, Richard led the batting. He was considered to be one of the best crick-eters among the younger pupils, for he had speed, bowling power and stamina, and was a strong and reliable bat. His batting was magnificent, and his score slowly mounted, much to the conster-nation of David's team. Thornley relieved Masefield at bowling because he was beginning to throw wild – De Macey's cold-shouldering of David had angered him, and he was taking the game in a personal way, greatly at the cost of his play. Richard took no chances now, for he had a healthy respect for the

Captain's fast deliveries. A yorker took him completely by surprise and, to avoid being hit, he whirled like a dervish, falling heavily on the ground as he lost his balance. From his position on the field, it looked to David that he had been struck on the temple, and he ran over to help him up.

'Are you all right?' he asked in natural concern for one who might be injured.

Richard frowned angrily and pushed him away.

'It's none of your business whether I am or not,' he replied roughly, and replaced his bat in the crease.

The incident affected his game. Throwing discretion to the winds, he played the bowling fiercely and freely, and, for a spell, made piecemeal of the sweating Thornley's deliveries. His innings ended when David, after a short sprint, caught the ball in his left hand. It hit his thumb and he dropped it, but, with the dexterity of a juggler, managed to catch it again in his right hand before it touched the ground. This splendid catch caught the imagination of the spectators, and cries of approval were uttered spontaneously by both teams. With an exclamation of extreme annoyance, Richard threw his bat on the ground. He picked it up again and walked towards the pavilion, a look of ill-concealed irritation on his face.

Thornley inspected David's hand.

'You've sprained your thumb, David, so you'd better call it a day. If we can't pull the fat out of the fire now, it won't be your fault.' He patted him in fatherly fashion on the shoulder. 'You've given yeoman service.'

After an unavailing protest, David left the field and followed the victim of his play into the pavilion. Richard frowned when he saw him come in. David sat down on one of the wooden benches and began nursing his sore finger under his armpit.

'It was a lucky catch,' Richard growled, but David was too busy with his sprain to take any notice of the remark. 'It served you jolly well right,' he went on hotly, angered by being ignored. 'You don't deserve any better luck.' David still refused to take the bait. 'I … I'm sorry, Madison,' he then confessed, ashamed of the brutal words he had spoken. 'I shouldn't have said that. I suppose it hurts awfully.'

David smiled over at him.

'It's not too bad now, thanks. It's stinging a bit, but it'll be all right in a few days.' He put on his blazer and, after gathering up and stowing his gear away, left the pavilion. Richard wished that he had stayed awhile so that he could have talked with him further. It was a new experience for him to admit a fault – and to Madison, of all people! He could not have explained at the time why he had done so, but he would grapple with the problem at a later date when he was in a better position to understand.

14

Coleman Wreaks Further Vengeance

In spite of the fine, sunny days of a promising summer, David thought that he noticed a hardly perceptible change in Tony's health. He was not really sure whether it was a fancy or not, for no one else observed anything amiss – not even the precocious Arthur. Nevertheless, he was inclined to put his faith in a sixth sense that all was not well with him. Showing no signs of recognizing any present or impending ailment himself, the subject of his concern acted with his accustomed fire and energy. Sometimes he looked a bit under the weather – at least, David thought so – but it was hard to say how great a part imagination played in the matter.

But there was something which the three friends did observe, something which was entirely unconnected with Tony's health. Richard De Macey was slowly modifying his deplorable attitude towards David. It wasn't so much what he did, as what he *didn't* do; not so much what he said, as what he left *unsaid*. The odious term of 'scholarship boy' dropped from his vocabulary, and he began to adopt a neutral attitude towards him, although Roye and Belford and their cronies kept up their taunting behaviour as before – when they judged it safe to do so.

Meanwhile, Coleman continued to plague the boys with little respite. One afternoon in class, before the master arrived, David handed an exercise book of Tony's, which he had been reading, back to him.

'You'd better keep this out of sight, Tony. If Coleman saw what you've written about him, all hell would break loose.'

'It's all true.'

'No one denies that,' Arthur said with a hoarse chuckle, having also read what was in it, 'but David's right. Put it away in a safe place or else destroy the evidence. We've had enough crises since we came back this term to last us a lifetime.'

What the obviously inflammatory contents penned by Tony in his exercise book might be intrigued his curious classmates, and the book began to circulate among the boys. There was much chuckling and cries of approval when they read what it contained, and his friends agreed that he was the ideal lampoonist for a brute like their master.

'By the way, Tony, how are you feeling now?' asked David. That day, his suspicions about the other's deterioration in health had been definitely confirmed. Since morning, Tony had felt sick and had vomited after one of his meals.

'Not very well. I'm a bit headachy on and off. I think I've felt something like this before since the holidays, but not so badly. My throat is a little sore as well.'

'I didn't know that you weren't feeling well,' Thornley remarked in commiseration. 'You're looking and acting chipper enough.'

Tony grinned.

'It's my great spirit that keeps me going. I'm a triumph of mind over matter. I'll probably be my old self by morning.'

'He vomited after lunch,' David told the boys. He was much more concerned about it all than was the sufferer himself.

'You're making a mountain out of a molehill, David. It's probably something I ate which didn't agree with me. In any case, I promise that I'll see Matron tomorrow if I'm feeling no better. And I always keep my word. You know that.'

David laughed.

'You're only waiting until tomorrow so that you can skip classes.'

'I don't blame him,' Thornley said. 'They're an ordeal these days.'

'I may as well make the most of it while I can. Talking about sickness – any more news about Mr Ledwidge, Arthur?'

Arthur looked at him in his most adult manner.

'Condition unchanged, Tony.'

'What *is* wrong with him?'

'You wouldn't understand the professional details – but he *is* very ill.'

There was no more time for chatting. Coleman burst into the room, gown flying, the door slapping against the wall with a crash. His face was as black as thunder, and it was soon apparent to the startled pupils that in his present foul temper no one would be immune from punishment if the occasion called for it; even Roye and his clique hardly dared to breathe in case his wrath descended upon their section of the class. Gilbert knew that the master's judgement was too clouded at the moment to separate the chaff from the wheat, as it were.

Coleman threw two exercise books at David and Thornley with such violence that they were unable to catch them.

'When I give you lines to do, I don't countenance mass-production work. You can do them over again, and this time I insist on copperplate writing. If you scribble again, I'll double the number.' He was silent for a moment or two, but everyone sensed that there was more trouble brewing. He began to pace the floor deliberately while the boys watched his every move like hawks. 'I'm afraid I'm dealing with a deceitful lot of boys. Do you know what I'm referring to, Thornley?'

'No, sir.' Thornley shook his head, but he guessed what he meant and steeled himself in preparation for the coming onslaught.

'You liar!' shouted Coleman. 'You are completely without honour. Do you imagine, for one instant, that you're dealing with a fool? Have you the stupidity to think that I don't realize what's been going on behind my back? What explanation have you to offer for arranging matches when I'm not present?' He was referring to those which the Captain had arranged on his own initiative so that the team could get more practical game play than Coleman officially sanctioned. They had been held as secretly as possible, but it had been a foregone conclusion that, sooner or later, Coleman would learn about them.

'We play them in our own time, sir. They don't interfere with *your* training methods.' Thornley realized, almost as soon as the words were out of his mouth, that his last remark was a dangerous thing to say with the master in his present foul temper, implying as it did, not just disapproval of them, but actual contempt for them. At the centre of Coleman's 'method' was running the boys about the school grounds until they were fit to drop.

'My methods aren't good enough for you? Is that what you mean to say?'

'We haven't been getting enough match play, sir,' Thornley parried, avoiding the question.

'You've played against selections from Abbot's. What more do you want?'

'When the school team plays against those who haven't an earthly of ever getting on it, that's no practice.'

'I suppose your stupid idea of mixing the teams is superior?'

'Yes, sir.' Thornley had crossed the Rubicon. 'Until I began to arrange my own matches we were only hanging on by the skin of our teeth in the Cup.' Easy-going as he was, he was prepared to fight the issue to the last and showed the stuff which made him such a sterling leader.

'You're a pig-headed, insubordinate fool. I'll tolerate no more of *your* training methods. One trainer will be quite sufficient for your precious team.'

No one will ever know where the verbal skirmish between Thornley and the master would have ended, because at that point Tony Masefield committed a fatal mistake which switched the master's attention in his direction. He nudged Arthur and whispered something to him, and Coleman saw him out of the corner of his eye.

'I didn't find your exercise book on my table, Masefield.'

Before an ashen-faced Tony could reply, disaster struck. The incriminating item in question had come into Roye's possession when it was being passed around just before Coleman stormed in, and Gilbert let it drop on the floor with an audible, muffled thud. This might have passed unnoticed, but Tony showed such obvious signs of distress that it immediately became the focal point of everyone's attention.

'Hand it to me, Roye.' Coleman fingered through the pages after it had been handed to him, and then inspected the cover to find the owner's name, but, fortunately, there was none. 'Did … did you write this … this pernicious poison, Masefield?' he demanded harshly, his face contorted with anger.

Tony was thoroughly scared. His brown eyes were wide with terror, and his slight body was trembling from head to foot.

'N-no, sir. It wasn't me.'

'Until the culprit confesses, no boy will leave this room,' the master told the frightened boys, surveying them grimly. Then, one by one, he questioned them in an endeavour to locate the guilty party. Answers in the negative, uttered in hoarse, stuttering, cowed, intimidated voices, greeted his query. 'Remember, I can find out who's responsible by the writing,' he warned them tersely, continuing with his interrogation. It came to David's turn. 'Did you write this, Madison?'

'Yes, sir,' David answered weakly, licking dry lips.

With long strides, Coleman went over to his desk, and towering over him, struck him mercilessly with his open hand across the face. The colour rushed into David's cheeks from the brutal assault.

'Stand out on the floor, you insolent puppy,' he roared, beside himself with fury. 'I'll teach you to disrespect me.' He picked up his cane and confronted the terrified boy.

Poor Tony! Too late did he see the awful consequences of his lie.

'I did it, sir,' he confessed in great torment of mind, leaving his bench and approaching the teacher in a state of terror. 'Madison had nothing to do with it.'

'Get back to your seat, you little nuisance. You had your chance to speak. You're becoming as big a pest as Madison.' He could not conceal his venom towards him because of his loyalty to David. 'I'll make an example of you, too, if I have any more of your nonsense.'

But Tony persisted bravely and caught the master's arm as he raised his cane to strike the supposed culprit.

'But I did do it. You've no right to punish him.' He was almost frantic to right the wrong.

Coleman flung him against a desk roughly.

'I've had about enough of your whining. Do as you're told, or I'll report you to the Headmaster.'

The unhappy Tony returned to his place, while the sadistic monster, firm of malevolent purpose, gave his full attention to his victim.

He brought the cane swishing down on the boy's outstretched hand a number of times, disregarding the nearness to the wrist of some of the strokes. 'The other hand, boy,' he roared, as cries of pain escaped David's white, tightened lips.

'Please, sir,' David protested almost inaudibly, continuing to hold out the same hand, 'I sprained my other thumb playing cricket.'

The master laughed harshly.

'Then perhaps this will cure it. Don't be stubborn, you puppy. Your hand!' David held out the hand with the injured finger, and Coleman caned him until he was sick with pain. 'That should help to improve your respect for your betters in future, Madison,' he shouted angrily when he had ended his brutal assault.

Somehow David managed to struggle back to his seat. The boys were shaken by his ordeal almost as much as he was, except for Roye and Belford, who were tittering and whispering together.

De Macey was frowning, for he was as shocked as the rest of the class by the vicious episode.

Because of his interruption, Tony was detained after class, and David slipped away to the dormitory since he didn't feel up to speaking to his commiserating friends. He was faint with pain, and sick with unhappiness. That was the worst beating Coleman had ever given him, and each time he secretly became more terrified of him.

Richard De Macey was passing the half-open door of the dormitory and stopped outside hesitantly. He took off his cap and twisted it in his hands. With much embarrassment, he awkwardly offered his sympathy.

'Coleman's an awful brute. It was frightfully brave what you did this afternoon. But why did you take the blame?' He searched the other's face keenly.

David summoned up a wan little smile.

'Tony hasn't been well all day, and he was sick after lunch. In any case, he's my best friend. He'd do the same for me.'

Roye and Belford came up the stairs, and they looked venomously at David. They, too, had noticed Richard's changing attitude towards him, and it was anathema to both of them.

'Are you coming down to the Common Room, Richard?' Roye demanded. 'Let Madison stew in his own juice.'

'I … I have to go now,' Richard explained in confusion, and followed the other two down the corridor.

David didn't go to dinner. To forget his troubles, he went rambling over the fields to Abbotmead. After a cup of tea and some sandwiches in his favourite teashop, he bought some pencils and notepaper in a nearby stationer's and faced school-wards again.

When he arrived back at Abbot's, Tony was waiting distract-edly for him in the dormitory. Tony had been crying before he came in, and, although he had endeavoured to remove all telltale signs, tear marks still streaked his cheeks. He blew his nose to stop the tears from flowing before attempting to speak.

'Are we still friends, David?' he asked anxiously, checking a sob.

'Of course we are, Tony. Why do you ask such a question?'

Tony choked back a huge sob.

'I thought you were trying to avoid me when you didn't come to dinner and didn't want to speak to me again.'

'Of course not. I walked to Abbeymead. I can't stand this place any more. It's becoming more and more like a dungeon every day. I can hardly remember how happy I was when Mr Ledwidge was here.' He was intensely moved by his friend's emotional upset, which was the result of his devotion to him, and he yearned to comfort Tony.

But Tony was inconsolable.

'I was nothing but a coward, and I let you down when you needed me most.'

'You told Coleman that you'd written about him, but he didn't want to listen. He was only looking for an excuse to vent his anger on me. He'd have given me a caning for something or other anyway.'

'I don't care. I was a coward and I'll never forgive myself. And I'll never forget you for taking the blame.' He still refused to be consoled. The incident had left a terrible, psychological mark, for he felt that he had betrayed his friend.

'Stop blaming yourself. You're sick enough as it is. You did everything you could.'

Tony's countenance brightened with hope.

'I know what I'll do. I'll go to the Doctor and explain every-thing.'

'That would do no good, Tony. You'd only get into unneces-sary trouble.'

'I don't care. The same could happen to you, David, without it being your fault.'

'I don't think Coleman will say anything to Dr Princeton. In any case, I'm as good as expelled already. Unless a miracle

happens, I'll be a goner after the meeting of the school Governors. Coleman has seen to that.'

'I'll pray for one,' promised the inconsolable boy, with tears
smarting in his eyes. If faith can move mountains, then the
miracle would surely happen. 'It's so unfair! It's so unfair! I'd
give my life for you,' he added, in a sudden, emotional outburst,
seeking to compensate for his mistaken cowardice.

'You risked your life for me once when you climbed up into
the clock tower during the snow. It couldn't have been more
dangerous at the time and you could easily have been killed.'

'You're only saying that to please me.'

'I'm not trying to please you, Tony,' David insisted. 'I'm saying
it because it's true. I'd never have been able to bear it here but
for you, especially, and my other friends.'

'Thanks, David.' Tony's soulful eyes looked gratefully into his.
He was a little lifted out of his depression by this timely reminder
of his bravery, and he smiled wanly; but further therapy was
needed to complete his rehabilitation into a more realistic frame
of mind.

In the dormitory that night, the boys knew that the day's
events would inevitably come up for comment, and everyone
waited expectantly for someone else to cast off first. It wasn't
David. He was too busy with his thoughts. Tony pretended to go
to sleep, but David could hear him quietly weeping, and his
compassion flowed out to him at this return of his morbid
depression.

'That was the worst rage I've ever seen the Beast in, David –
he was almost frothing at the mouth,' Thornley commented,
sitting up in bed and starting the ball rolling 'He certainly took it
out on you. If I had kept my big mouth shut, he mightn't have
gone quite so berserk. But I just couldn't give a hoot what I said.
He's done all he can to ruin our chances in the Cup.'

'You told him the truth, Thornley,' David answered. 'It was
worth it to see his face when you gave him a taste of his own
medicine.'

'It was your fault, Roye,' exclaimed the Captain angrily, turning in Gilbert's direction. 'You as good as gave Coleman the exercise book.'

'That's a lie! You're trying to make a martyr out of Madison at my expense. I couldn't help it.' He was alarmed and infuriated by the accusation. He had thought that his evil, deliberate act had escaped detection, and, like a cornered animal, he was prepared to fight and justify himself by whatever means he could.

'I saw you drop it, you mangy beggar. You couldn't have done it if you hadn't wanted to.'

'It was an accident, you liar. Belford will tell you it was.'

'No one would accept his word for anything,' piped up one of the younger boys from the depths of his pillow. 'He's as big a liar as you are.'

'You mind what you're saying,' roared Belford angrily, touched on the raw, 'or I'll make you eat your words.'

The other laughed contemptuously.

'You're only a cheat and a fraud. David spiked your guns good and proper and showed you up for the cowardly bully that you are.'

'Masefield's the coward,' Gilbert accused wildly, shifting to another tactic as he sought to extricate himself from the web of guilt which the others were weaving about him. 'He let Madison take his punishment for him. The scholarship boy has only got himself to blame for trying to be a hero. He's nothing but a fool, and Mr Coleman only gave him what he deserves. He was always a troublemaker, and he shouldn't be in the school. If I'm wrong, let them speak for themselves.'

Howls of indignation and wrath rent the air at these vicious untruths.

'Nobody believes your dirty insults, Roye,' Thornley told him, 'and no one with a grain of sense would bother to refute them.'

Belford sneered. 'Gilbert's right. Masefield showed the white feather. He's Madison's friend until it has to be proved.'

David still kept silent. He was too sick of the entire business to answer the scurrilous charges. When the iconoclasts had referred to Masefield's supposed cowardice, Tony had begun weeping afresh, and David could see his slight form heaving as he muffled his sobs. After a short, charged interval, during which Roye and Belford occupied themselves with sneering and snickering, to the great provocation of the other boys, the clear voice of Richard De Macey spoke up, and the dormitory immediately became hushed to hear what he had to say.

'I'm no friend of Masefield's, and I never was,' he stated deliberately, having considered the text of his utterance very carefully, 'but he's no coward …'

'What are you saying, Richard?' cried Roye in astonishment, never expecting a refutation of his charge of cowardice from his closest friend. 'You must be crazy.'

'Shut up and let De Macey speak,' a voice ordered peremptorily.

'Masefield's no coward, and he never was. We all know that.' There were cries of agreement with, and approval of, this honest opinion from every corner of the dormitory, and Tony suddenly stopped weeping in order to listen. 'Coleman was almost insane with fury this afternoon. If any of us had written the things about him that Masefield did, we'd all have denied it. I dare anyone to deny that.' He paused for a rebuttal, but there was none, everyone remaining silent. 'But there's no telling how many of us would have had the pluck, like Masefield, to try and put things right when another shouldered the blame. Coleman knew he'd done it – I bet he recognized the handwriting immediately – but it made no difference. He's had it in for Madison since he came to the Abbey. As for Madison, he did what none of us would ever have the courage to do.'

'Hear! Hear!' agreed Thornley, and, except for Roye's cronies, all of the other boys chimed in.

'Whose side are you on?' Gilbert asked angrily. 'Theirs or ours?'

'It's not a question of sides, Gilbert,' was the quiet, but firm, reply. 'It's a question of truth and lies. Did you mean for Coleman to get the exercise book?'

With eyes ablaze like an animal's, the other turned on him savagely.

'Are you believing those liars instead of me?'

'I only asked you a simple question. You needn't bite my head off.'

Gilbert realized that he was showing the cloven hoof. He valued Richard's friendship more than that of all his other friends put together, and it was too precious to risk losing.

'Of course not, Richard,' he answered, in a more subdued tone. 'It was an accident. You believe me, don't you?' There was no answer. 'You believe me, don't you?' he asked a second time, keeping his temper under control with a great effort.

'Shut up and go to sleep,' Richard told him. It was a partially effective order, for the angry Roye, thinking better than to attempt any further queries on the subject, sulked in silence.

When the lights went out, low voices commented upon Richard's superb summing-up of the incident, and much admiration was expressed at his honesty and fairness towards his clique's adversaries. Eventually, one by one, the boys began dropping off to sleep, contented now that the ridiculous charges against their two friends had been well and truly refuted.

Roye and Belford were simmering with resentment towards Richard, and fuming impotently because their baseless slanders and lies had hopelessly misfired – until they, too, dropped off to sleep. But three boys still lay awake, and their thoughts were very similar in many ways.

15

The Thoughts of Three Boys

Tony Masefield was thinking about De Macey's totally unexpected rebuttal of the baseless charge of cowardice which had been made against him, a rebuttal to which he had listened with gratitude. David had said almost the same thing earlier in the day, but coming as it did from one who was no friend of his, it carried a far greater weight – he knew that David wouldn't have said anything to hurt him, anyway, whatever the circumstances – and provided that extra psychological lift which he needed to make him see the incident in the right perspective. However, despite his return to spiritual peace, he wasn't feeling too well. His throat felt as if there was something pressing on it from behind, and things were beginning to take on a dreamlike quality. He said a little prayer asking that his condition improve by morning, then, snuggling well down between the sheets, he drifted off into a fitful sleep.

David had welcomed Richard's declaration about Tony's courage much more than the flattering compliment which he himself had been paid because he had accepted the blame. Its essential decency had cheered him, and taught him that, however black some people appeared, there was often a good side to their natures. The distress shown by Tony in the dormitory earlier in the day had affected him more than anything in his life before, and the deep affection it indicated was a staff to sustain him in the trials yet to come. He thanked God for giving him such a lovable, loyal companion, who had proved his willingness to stand by him on every occasion when that had been demanded of him. Next, he pondered upon his own position. It was only a matter of time before he would be expelled from the school, which at one time had promised so much future happiness. But his parents were his greatest worry. He dreaded their disappointment and the dashing of their hopes when they learned of his coming expulsion, and their shock would be all the greater since they could suspect nothing of the impending event. Even now, David knew that he would do the same again – conceal the true position as long as possible to spare them pain – had he to live through things a second time. He was, however, determined not to leave St Donat's, as Coleman had once put it, 'like a whipped cur with his tail between his legs'. He turned wearily on his side and contemplated the gloomy outlook until heavy lids closed mercifully over sleep-laden eyes.

Richard De Macey, a concentrated expression on his face, and his hands joined behind his head on the pillow, lay awake long after the other boys had gone to sleep. He was oblivious of the quiet breathing of the sleepers, and he hardly heard the occasional creaking of springs as a boy changed his position in bed. He had never come so near to philosophizing, and some of his thoughts hurt. His father's advice at the beginning of the school year came back to him: 'Choose your companions wisely. A worthwhile friend, who can influence you for the good, is an inestimable blessing.' He recalled how petulantly he had forced an end to the talk, treating the well-meaning concern of his parent in a disrespectful and ill-mannered way. He considered his associates in general, and Gilbert Roye, in particular, since he was a crude distillation of the lot. Roye was snobbish and mean. Although liberally supplied with pocket money and material perquisites of every kind, he never bought anything that could be cadged and seldom gave anything to anyone except as a bribe or to solicit favours. He displayed his true colours by the way he treated David – with snobbishness, contempt and vindictiveness, and completely without any regard for his feelings. He was also vicious and cruel, streaks in his nature which he had adequately demonstrated when he and Richard and the others had attacked David during the first term. The complexion he had tried to put on the afternoon's episode, with implications of cowardice on Masefield's part, and vainglory on David's, had so disgusted him that he had been forced to give the well-received rebuttal.

In contrast, there was David. Except for himself and his cronies – and, of course, Coleman – he was popular with every-body. Richard examined in his mind the reasons for his popularity. Quiet and even-tempered, he was always ready to join in a laugh or a game, or help his friends when they needed it. His was a position among the boys that no amount of rank or money could buy. How he had stood up to Belford, and that afternoon to the despicable Coleman – both times on Masefield's behalf – Richard could not but admire now. He was beginning to understand that he and Roye and the others were really the outcasts, and the tragedy of it was that they revelled in their peculiar exclusiveness with a ludicrous sense of superiority and pride. David had never done anything to merit their callous treatment of him, which was rooted in snobbery and all the worst traits. He had suffered the humiliations bravely and had never shown any resentment. Indeed, he had even been concerned that time at cricket when he thought that Richard had been struck dangerously by the ball. How often had he, Richard, taken such displays of concern and character as signs of inferiority and weakness! How lamentably had his ideas become corrupted due to constant contact with low standards of thought and conduct!

He next focused his mind on Coleman. He was old enough to realize that the master considered David fair game for his sadistic bent, since, being a free pupil – hence a nobody in Coleman's opinion – he had no cause for complaint no matter how badly he was treated. That was also his friends' credo, too. He had to confess, with a shudder, that early on he had welcomed the master just as much as they had, as another agent for heaping further ignominies on their unfortunate victim.

Finally, he considered the occasions on which he had shown some sparks of decency in his relations with David. He doubted whether he could take full credit for stopping Belford and his clique from attacking him after the fight during the snow. Then, he would just as happily have watched him being thrashed in single combat, but whatever sense of fair play he possessed had revolted when they were about to take him at a numerical disadvantage. Twice he had displayed real compassion and sympathy: in the pavilion after David had sprained his thumb playing cricket; again, after the fiendish caning that afternoon. He felt that was his true self. He had faced up to himself for the first time in his life without trying to make allowances and excuses for his many faults. With a deep sigh, he dropped off to sleep ...

16

'The Witching Time of Night'

Something woke David late that night, and he wondered dreamily what it could be. The weather had changed during his first sleep; before, it had been blustery but dry; now he could hear the wind soughing mournfully around the gables of Abbot's House and rain spattering in heavy drops against the dormitory windows. He was about to conclude that he had been roused by the wind and rain, when a sudden, peculiar, smothered groan from Tony's bed made him sit up with a jerk. He wondered if he was having a nightmare, but then a throaty, gurgling sound followed the other, and something like a protest came from his friend.

'Tony!' he called softly so as not to disturb the other sleepers, but there was no response. His eyes were becoming accustomed to the darkness now, but apart from the dim figure in the bed he could discern no details. He stretched out his hand and put it on the other's pillow. He drew it back quickly, for it had touched a warm, sticky fluid. Thoroughly alarmed, he called to Tony more loudly, but except for gasping breathing and smothered groans, which were now becoming frequent, there was still no answer. He slipped out of bed and went over to Tony's bed to see what the matter was.

De Macey had awakened and was looking at him sleepily. 'Is there anything wrong, Madison?' he inquired lazily, stifling a yawn with the back of his hand.

'I'm not sure yet,' David replied, glad to have some support in his investigation.

He switched on the night light near Tony's bed, and the colour left his cheeks at what he saw. Tiredness gone, Richard jumped out of bed and joined him at Masefield's bedside, his expression as frightened and as horrified as his. The pillow and sheets of Tony's bed were saturated with coagulating blood. It had come from Tony's mouth, and the startled boys could see that, still dribbling in trickles from its corners, was a frothy mixture of air and brighter blood. His face was ashen, and his thin body gave an occasional toss as huge sighs made his chest heave.

Tony was literally fighting for his life. He opened his eyes and looked up into David's white face. 'I'm so cold … I'm so cold …' he cried in a weak voice which trailed off.

'Don't try to speak, Tony,' David whispered hoarsely. 'Will you get some blankets, De Macey? You'll find some in the hot press at the top of the stairs.'

'Righto, Madison!' Richard answered in a small voice and, without wasting another second, raced noiselessly out of the dormitory.

'I won't die, will I, David?' asked Tony pathetically, trying to sit up.

Kneeling at the side of his bed, David gently restrained him.

'No, Tony,' he assured him, with a sob in his voice and with a tone of conviction that he didn't really feel, 'you won't die.'

However, this response seemed to comfort the ailing boy. His eyes closed and his head lolled over to one side. 'I'm so cold … I'm so cold …' His voice grew weaker as he became comatose.

Richard came running back carrying an armful of blankets. 'How is he now?' he asked in a hushed tone.

'He's become unconscious.' They covered Tony with the blankets as gently as they could. 'I'll get Matron,' he whispered to Richard when that was done. 'You stay here. If he wakes up, he may try to get up, but don't let him.'

'I won't.' Richard sat at the side of the patient to keep vigil, and didn't dare move a muscle in case any movement might do harm.

None of the others in the dormitory had woken up, for the two boys had been as quiet as possible, and the light which had been switched on barely illuminated their surroundings. David put on his shoes and dressing gown and – after a last wide-eyed look at the figure in the bed, and then at Richard, who gave him a weak smile – tiptoed out.

Holding his breath fearfully, he crept slowly down the corridor, which was but dimly lit, and reached the top of the staircase without mishap. Gripping the banisters tightly, he went down the stairs very carefully, one step at a time. He ran down another corridor where it was less dark. He could hear the branches of trees scraping and knocking against the windowpanes, which, in his present pent-up state of mind, sounded as if some unknown horrors were trying to gain entry. His heart almost stopped beating when he came to the next staircase. From the hall below, after a protesting whirr of machinery, the old grandfather clock struck the hour of midnight. It was now the 'witching time of night', and suddenly, the full significance and associations of the time burst upon him.

Every story he had heard about the ghost-ridden abbey – particularly the one about the Abbot – flooded into his mind. With fear clutching icily at his breast, he descended the stairs, the eerie creaking of the old woodwork sending cold shivers up and down his spine. Gaining the hall, he swung back the heavy door, flew through Cloister Passage, then through Great Cloister, and crossed Cloister Court as fast as his trembling legs could carry him. The wind was blowing more fiercely now, but, mercifully, the rain had stopped. He knocked loudly on Matron's door. Soon a light appeared in one of the windows, and a few seconds later the door was opened by that buxom lady. Her hair was arranged in a sleeping plait and she was clad in a scarlet dressing gown, looking for all the world like a prizefighter.

'Good heavens, child!' she exclaimed, regarding her breathless caller with amazement. 'Why are you out of your bed at this hour of night? Whatever is the matter?' Solicitously, she hustled him indoors and closed the door.

Feeling safe from the terrors of the night for the moment, David explained the reason for his nocturnal visit, the words tumbling out in a cascade. She put on a coat over her dressing gown and picked up her first-aid kit. She showed him where the telephone was and told him to call Dr Gillespie and an ambulance while she went to see the patient. Then, with a reassuring smile, she was gone, and her hurrying footsteps were soon drowned out by the roaring of the wind.

When he had made his phone calls, David braced himself for the return journey to Abbot's. He raced back across Cloister Court, and there, no more than twenty yards away, he saw him. With a cry of terror, he recognized the Abbot. There was no mistaking him. The phantom stood there for a few seconds, illuminated by the moon which had broken through the clouds, giving David such a clear view of him that he knew it wasn't just a trick of the imagination. Tall and well built, with a moustache and beard, and wearing a cowl or hood over his head, and with his hands hidden in the folds of his habit, his two coal-black eyes were staring fixedly at him. Then the moon clouded over, and he was gone.

David's legs had turned to water and a cold sweat had broken out on his brow. In fearful dread, and pursued by all the spooks, goblins and flibbertigibbets of the night – or so he thought – he fled for his life from Cloister Court and then through Great Cloister and Cloister Passage into Abbot's House, and flew up the stairs to the dormitory, fearing a reappearance of the apparition elsewhere.

Matron had already cleaned Tony's ashen face clear of blood and had wrapped him in some fresh blankets which Richard had brought from the hot press.

'He's not quite so poorly now, dear,' she told David, seeing the question in his eyes.

Most of the other boys were now wide awake and were

watching Matron with frightened eyes as she expertly finished her work. A car came to a screeching halt outside, followed almost immediately by the sound of another vehicle. Dr Gillespie and the ambulance had arrived. Dr Gillespie came panting up the stairs and into the dormitory, his face as red as a beetroot and sweating profusely with exertion – such critical emergencies not being an everyday occurrence in his practice. Behind him were two ambulance men carrying a stretcher, and behind them, again, came Dr Princeton and Coleman. The last two were only partially dressed and had overcoats over their nightclothes.

Dr Gillespie felt Tony's pulse and forehead, and shone a torch into his mouth to inspect it. He next listened to his chest with a stethoscope and quickly finished his examination,

'We'll have to rush him to hospital,' he told the adults generally. 'He'll need a blood transfusion tonight. I think that something like an abscess has burst behind his throat and eroded a blood vessel.'

'Tony wasn't feeling well all day, Doctor,' David told him, greatly concerned about his stricken friend. 'His throat was sore as well.'

The doctor patted him on the head.

'Don't worry about him, David. He's in good hands now.' He turned to Matron. 'He is fairly stable at the moment.'

The ambulance men, under the doctor's supervision, lifted the still patient onto the stretcher, and they all went out except Matron. With an expertise born of long practice, she stripped the bed and removed the sheets and blankets, and soon not a trace of blood betrayed the fact that an emergency had just occurred. When she had done that, she smiled at the two boys who had taken such a big part in the affair, and then bustled out of the dormitory. David and Richard were too shocked to speak. There were tears in David's eyes, and he rubbed them away with his fingers. He recalled what Tony had said when he had been displaying his new garters before the Easter holidays: 'I swear that you'll never find me outside the dormitory in my right senses after lights out.' And now his words had come true.

He could hardly believe that he was gone. It was so much like a dream that, were it not for the evidence of the empty bed, white and tidy after Matron's ministrations, he would have thought nothing had happened. But gone he was, and a terrible ache filled his heart. He had lost his greatest friend and ally in the school. Physically, Tony may not have been more than a slip of a boy, but he had twined himself so inextricably about David's affections that life didn't seem possible without him. David prayed that he wouldn't … He was afraid to say the dreadful word and prayed all the harder. 'No, dear God! Not Tony!'

Soon afterwards, Dr Princeton came back again and regarded the two stricken boys kindly.

'The prompt action you've just taken is very commendable, Madison. You also deserve much credit for your help, De Macey. Dr Gillespie told me that if the poor boy had had a second haemorrhage during the night, without a blood transfusion, he would certainly have died.'

'Then he won't die now, sir?' David asked, his spirits lightening.

'No, Madison, he won't die now, thanks to you. The danger is past, thank God! I am told that he will be with us again before the end of the term.' David bit his lip and looked away. He would probably be expelled by then. The Headmaster, guessing correctly what was running through his mind, regretted his unintentional slip. 'About reporting you at the Governors' meeting – I'll have to take tonight's fine action into account, and I intend to give you a second chance.'

'Thank you, sir!' David said gratefully. Paradoxically, Tony's prayer for a miracle had been partly answered, for he had been granted a temporary reprieve. Although it was not a full miracle, it had been gained almost at the expense of Tony's death. He had offered to give his life for him if that were ever necessary not many hours before, and the fact of the matter was that he had very nearly done so.

'You realize that it's all up to you? I implore you to exploit this opportunity to the full.'

'Yes, sir.' There was little hope in his voice, for Coleman was the deciding factor, not himself. Still, he was grateful to the Headmaster for showing such concern about him. In spite of everything, Dr Princeton represented all that was good and kind in his estimation, and he laid no blame at his door for anything that had happened.

'I hope neither of you catches cold. Goodnight, boys!'

'Goodnight, sir!' chorused the two boys as the Headmaster left the dormitory.

'I'm glad Masefield's out of danger,' Richard said awkwardly. 'I wouldn't like to see anything happen to him.'

David sighed.

'Poor Tony! I can hardly believe he's gone. I'll miss him terribly.' His heart was nearly breaking.

'The Doctor said he'll be back before the end of the term.'

'I probably won't be here then and will never see him again.'

'You're not being reported to the Governors yet. Something may happen to change everything. Coleman just couldn't be allowed to carry on as he's doing. I wish I could help you.'

David smiled sadly at him.

'Thanks, De Macey! But it's no use. There's nothing anyone can do. I've given up hoping long ago. Anyway, I don't care about being expelled now. I hate St Donat's. Coleman has made my life a misery here.'

Richard coughed. He was all too conscious of his own part in the other's unhappiness.

'Why don't your parents do something about it?'

'I've told them nothing. I was hoping that Mr Ledwidge would come back in the meantime. In any case, I didn't want to worry them.'

Across the dormitory, Roye and Belford were whispering

together. They were clearly angered by this further friendly advance on Richard's part, and their venomous looks at David boded ill. By hook or by crook, they would hasten his downfall if it was the last thing they did.

Coleman came storming into the dormitory.

'Get back into your beds at once,' he barked, and pyjama-clad boys, who were talking in pairs and groups about the emergency, clambered back hastily between their sheets. Those who were propped up on their elbows in bed lowered themselves down, and, while pretending to go to sleep, eyed the unwelcome intruder warily.

'Which of you two went for Matron?' he demanded, addressing David and Richard.

'I did, sir,' answered David, after putting his dressing gown away.

'Why didn't you call me first?'

'There was no time, sir.'

'I see,' murmured the master with dangerous calm. 'Not satisfied with the way things are run here, you've decided to run them your own way, is that it?'

'No, sir,' protested David. 'I thought it best.'

'You did, eh?' The storm broke. 'You ill-bred wretch,' the master roared in a temper, working himself up into one of his frightening furies. 'I'll teach you to go over my head.' He hit the defenceless boy on the face and David went reeling on to the floor. He struck the back of his head on the corner of a radiator and lay there in a dazed condition. 'If I catch you out of bed again tonight, I'll flay you alive.' He turned to Richard, who was now in bed. 'I thought you had more sense, De Macey, than to be gallivanting about when you should be asleep.' He switched off the lights and stalked angrily out of the dormitory.

Leaving the sanctuary of his bed, Richard jumped onto the floor and went to David's aid. He helped him up and assisted him back into bed.

'He's an awful brute. Did you hurt yourself, Madison?'

'Not much. I've got a bit of a bump on my head, that's all,' David replied, feeling it. 'It's nothing serious, though.'

'We'd better be getting back into bed in case he comes back. It's the sort of sneaky thing he'd do. Goodnight, Madison!'

'Goodnight, De Macey!'

They both scampered back into their beds, and the two boys fell into an exhausted sleep as soon as their heads touched their pillows. The night had given both of them one of the most memorable experiences of their lives.

17

Roye and Belford Hatch a Plot

David wrote a sad little letter home telling them about Tony's illness. He also received one from Tony's parents a few days later. They wrote that their son was progressing favourably, that he would write himself when he was a little better, that he would be returning to school in a month or so – David swallowed hard at this painful reminder of his precarious tenure at St Donat's – and that only for him Tony would not be alive. They concluded by saying that they'd be forever in his debt and that they owed him their son. The letter pleased him very much, but he wasn't too sure what the last bit meant.

Meanwhile, Roye and Belford were plotting together to cause him whatever further trouble they could. Richard's ever-increasing courtesies towards him alarmed them very much more than his previous neutral attitude towards him had done. Richard was also cooling towards them as well. He had not actually broken with them, for as yet he wasn't certain where his real loyalties lay. Roye, however, guessed that it was only a matter of time before he threw them over, and that David's continued presence in the school was a constant threat to their security and unity. Something had to be done and done quickly. Time was the essence of the contract. The two conspirators, having nothing more worthwhile on their agenda, as usual, were discussing the situation in the hall of Abbot's one sunny after-noon.

'Richard is becoming too friendly with Madison,' Gilbert was saying. 'He'll be a chum of his someday if we don't do something about it.'

'He only speaks to him now and then, Gilbert. I don't see what harm that can do. In any case, he knows we wouldn't have anything to do with Madison. Madison knows it, too.' He guffawed loudly as if he had said something clever.

'Go ahead and laugh. Unless you're blind, you must have noticed how he treats him now – as if he were an equal. Mr Coleman has seen the change as well. He gave him lines to do again yesterday.'

'Richard wouldn't throw us over for the likes of Madison,' exclaimed Belford disbelievingly. 'You're batty!'

'Don't be too sure about that. He resents it if we pass any unpleasant remarks about him. You've noticed that much at least?'

'Yes, I have,' the other said slowly, giving the matter more consideration than he had been doing. 'But what can we do about it?'

'There must be something. Madison would have been kicked out of the school weeks ago if Masefield's illness hadn't torn everything.'

'With luck, it won't be long now. The Doctor won't keep the little tramp here for ever on account of that.'

Gilbert laughed tauntingly.

'I bet you'll be glad when he's gone. He made you a right laughing stock last term. As long as he's at the Abbey, you'll never be able to live that down. His friends won't let you forget it in a hurry.'

The taunt stung – as it was intended to – and Belford reddened angrily.

'I got no help from you. You took good care to let me do the fighting.'

It was Roye's turn to lose his temper.

'I would have helped you but for Richard. He stopped me from backing you up.'

'You're such an obedient boy!' was the sarcastic retort to that weak excuse.

'That's when he began to change towards Madison. It's more your fault than mine.'

'What's the use of talking about the past. It gets us nowhere.'

In a sulky mood, Belford began walking about the hall and stopped at the table near the grandfather clock to examine two parcels which were on it. One was addressed to Madison; the other to Mr Coleman.

'I wonder what Madison's getting a parcel for at this stage?'

Gilbert went over to him.

'What's in it? Tuck?'

Belford felt the contours of one of the parcels and tested its weight.

'No. Books, I imagine. This one's for Mr Coleman,' he said, picking up the other one and inspecting the label. 'It has books in it, too, I'd say. I heard him ask the porter if a parcel had come for him from London. This must be it. There's a London post-mark on the stamps.' He screwed up his eyes to try to discover where the one he had in his hands came from. 'I can't make out where this one's from. The label is plain, and the postmarks are too smudgy. It would serve Madison right if we hid Mr Coleman's parcel among his things. He'd be given a thundering good hiding then.' He brayed loudly like the jackass that he was. 'It would be the price of the blighter,' he growled vindictively. 'But Madison would never do such a thing. No one would believe he had done it.'

Gilbert took great exception to this statement, since it implied that David would never stoop to do any despicable action, let alone steal what belonged to another. A repulsive sneer spread over his pudgy countenance.

'And why not? Because he's such a model little boy?'

'I didn't mean that, and you know it.'

But Gilbert was not the kind to give up so easily. 'If only we could get him to take it himself ...' An idea was beginning to take shape in his scheming brain. At last he had it.

'There's one way that could be managed, Belford,' he said slowly.

'How?'

'Suppose we were to put Madison's label on Mr Coleman's parcel? What do you think would happen?'

'Madison would take the wrong one, of course. I'm not stupid. But what about Madison's parcel? Would we put Mr Coleman's label on that?'

'You're a bigger ass than I imagined. We'd have to get rid of it somewhere, or else destroy it. There must be no evidence that Madison was ever sent a parcel.'

'I see now what you mean. But it sounds very risky.' Belford didn't like risks. Since his fight with David, he had become even more wary of unknown odds. The stratagem sounded good in theory – and he wasn't adverse to its probable consequences on their enemy – but he was afraid of a possible backfire.

'Not afraid of being caught, are you?'

'I won't show the white feather if you don't. I want to even scores with Madison just as much as you do.'

'Then it's settled. Here, give me a hand to untie the twine on the labels.' They each took a parcel and, untying the labels, exchanged them as planned. 'Take Madison's parcel and put it away in the cupboard below the stairs. We'll decide what to do with it later.' Belford left him to do as he was told. 'Remember, Richard's not to hear anything about this,' Gilbert warned when he had returned from his assignment. 'He mightn't side with us against Madison now.'

'He won't hear anything from me. Look out, someone's coming.'

They both stood well away from the table and as nonchalantly as possible pretended to be deep in conversation. Richard came into the hall wearing his cap and blazer.

'Hello, Richard!' said Roye in greeting. 'We're going over to Abbeymead later. Will you come?'

'I can't, Gilbert.'

'You mean you *won't*. Why can't you?'

'If you must know, I'm doing some practice at the nets in about half an hour.'

'Thornley's got you tied to his apron strings,' Gilbert commented sarcastically. 'Why don't you admit that he asked you to practise. First, rugger, now cricket. You'll be knitting sweaters for the team next.'

Belford considered this an excellent jest and bellowed raucously with laughter. But Richard remained unruffled.

'You can think what you like. That's your privilege. But it would be better if the pair of you began to take some interest in something instead of wasting your time jeering at other people.'

'Don't be touchy. I was only joking. We'll wait for you.'

'I still can't go. I've loads of study to do afterwards. It's been piling up on me.'

'I remember you boasting once that you hadn't to worry about studying. You said that you wouldn't have to work for a living.'

'I've changed my mind.'

Gilbert laughed mirthlessly and turned to Belford.

'You'd think Richard was studying for a scholarship. We'll have two scholarship boys in Abbot's before we're finished.'

'Shut up, Gilbert,' Richard said. 'You're not the least bit funny.' He spotted the parcel on the table. 'Who's the parcel for?'

'It's …' began Belford, but Gilbert cut in quickly.

'How should we know? We don't work for the Post Office.'

'You mustn't be as curious as you were. It could be for one of you.' He went over to the table and, after looking at the label, picked it up.

'What do you think you're doing with it?' Belford asked unthinkingly. 'It's not for you.'

Richard looked questioningly from Belford to Roye.

'I thought you didn't know whom it's for? I'm passing the

study and I may as well drop it in there for Madison. I saw him there a short time ago. Have you any objections?'

'No,' replied Gilbert sourly, 'but you're becoming too pally with him. We were all much happier before he came to the school. He's coming between us.'

'I'll be as friendly with him as I please,' Richard answered, clearing his throat. 'You can like it or lump it.' He left them abruptly and went upstairs.

'That wasn't such a bright idea after all,' Belford remarked disparagingly. 'We don't want to fall out with Richard.'

'How was I to know he'd walk in?'

Just at that moment, Coleman came out of his room. He looked towards the table and then spoke to Belford.

'I believe there's a parcel for me here. Did you see one, Belford?'

'Yes, sir. There was one for you on the table a while ago.' He ignored Gilbert's angry look of warning. 'Wasn't there, Gilbert?'

Gilbert nodded dumbly, and the master looked towards the table again.

'Well, Belford, where is it? I can't stand here talking all day.'

'I saw Madison with it, sir. I think he took it to the study.'

'I'll soon see about that,' Coleman said grimly and strode very purposefully out of the hall to go there.

Gilbert turned furiously on his accomplice.

'You're a stupid fool, Belford. You've as good as given the game away.'

'What do you mean – I've given it away? I said nothing I shouldn't have.'

'First, you as good as told Richard that we knew there was a parcel for Madison, and now you tell Coleman that Madison took his.'

'I told you that it was a risky business. I didn't want to get mixed up in it.'

'You liar!' shouted Roye, red-faced with rage. 'But you're in it now as much as I am, and you needn't try to wriggle out of it. Every time you open your mouth you put your foot in it.'

Judging it wise to get rid of the remaining evidence, the two plotters retrieved the second parcel from the cupboard where it had been put and took it to the boiler room with the intention of burning it. To their annoyance, the furnace wasn't lit, so they covered it up with an old piece of sacking, planning to destroy it at the earliest opportunity.

18

Richard Accuses the Plotters

Richard delivered the parcel to David in the study, with a good deal of embarrassment, admittedly, but when he had done so he felt pleased with himself. Sometime later, when he was passing through the hall, he was dumbfounded to see him coming out of Coleman's room, his body convulsed with suppressed crying. He concluded that he had suffered yet another punishment at the hands of the tyrant. He tried to offer his sympathy, but David brushed past him, his eyes, suffused with blinding tears, giving him an accusing look; and he was gone before he could recover from his bewilderment. He met Roye and Belford in Cloister Passage a few minutes later.

'What's wrong, Richard?' Gilbert enquired uneasily, quick to notice his air of preoccupation.

'Coleman's given Madison another thrashing just now.'

'That's nothing to do with us. You don't expect us to cry over him, do you?'

'Why should you worry your head about him?' Belford asked. 'He's never done anything for you.'

'Belford's right,' Gilbert agreed, backing him up. 'But you owe a lot to Mr Coleman. He's always easy on us.'

'That's no credit to us,' Richard stated flatly. 'I want no favours from the Beast in future. I'm fed up with his tyranny.'

'You didn't always think like this. We don't have to crawl before him.'

Richard grunted bitterly.

'We've been crawling on our bellies so long that we don't know what it feels like to stand on our feet like the rest of the class. The others have too much self-respect to curry favours.'

'You make me laugh! You want us all to be saints, now that you're trying to be one.'

'My eyes have been opened, and I can thank Madison for that.'

Before they could continue their rather bitter conversation, Coleman, with a triumphant look on his face, came out of his room.

'Madison took my parcel all right,' he told the boys, smirking. 'He won't touch other people's property again, I can assure you.'

'There was a parcel here for Madison,' Richard informed him, smelling a rat.

The master looked at him sharply.

'Watch your tone when you speak to me, De Macey. Your attitude recently has been just as reprehensible as that of others I could mention. What do you know about it?'

'There was one on the table and I brought it up to him. Did he not tell you – sir?'

'He mumbled something to that effect, but I fail to see how that alters the situation. He had my parcel, and there's an end to it.'

'But it was labelled to him – sir.'

Coleman regarded Richard as if he were dealing with a simpleton.

'You're a difficult boy to convince, De Macey. Madison was probably up to one of his usual monkey tricks and wrote the label himself. As we are all aware, by past experience, he is very proficient with the pen. There was a parcel addressed to me, wasn't there, Belford?'

'Y-yes, sir,' Belford confirmed shiftily.

'There, De Macey! That should convince even you. With a look of triumph at Richard, he swung on his heel and returned to his room.

Richard faced the other two angrily.

'What do you two know about this?'

'What should we know about it?' Belford replied, avoiding his eye. 'We're as much in the dark as you are. Madison must have swiped the parcel and written his own label, like Mr Coleman said.'

'Tell that to the marines. I thought you were hiding something from me when I saw you earlier. Belford has tied himself up in knots with his lies, and you needn't try to deny it. I'm finished with the pair of you for good.'

A desperate remedy being required for a desperate situation, Gilbert used a potent one in order to keep his friendship.

'Belford only meant it as a joke, Richard.'

'You're trying to put the whole blame on me,' Belford exclaimed wrathfully. 'You suggested it, not me.'

'He's trying to save his own skin,' Gilbert cried frantically, trying to strengthen his false allegation. 'Don't believe him.'

Richard looked contemptuously at both of them.

'Thornley and the others are right. You're liars, as well as everything else, and haven't got the guts to stand up for one another.'

When he had finished speaking, he turned on his heel and left them. He realized now the kind of company he had been keeping, and he was thankful that he had broken with them, before he, too, was swallowed up in their decadent moral quagmire. He went upstairs to look for David, but he wasn't in the study. He next went upstairs to the dormitory. He was anxious to find him, for he knew now the reason for his accusing expression and was eager to put things right.

David was lying face down on his bed crying, his spirit almost broken. On hearing footsteps, he raised himself up on an elbow and looked over his shoulder. His eyes had in them a depth of pain that Richard had never seen in anyone's eyes before.

'Why don't you leave me alone?' he cried in agony, gulping back his tears. 'I've never done anything to any of you.'

Richard fell back as if struck by a whiplash, the colour draining from his cheeks. The heart-rending appeal frightened him, but in a way quite different from the way he had felt during Tony Masefield's emergency. That was a situation he could cope with to a certain extent, being something of a physical nature. But the present situation was so overlaid with a psychological element, which, being so young, he couldn't really understand, that he was totally shattered by it – for all the anguish and pain of the insults and humiliations which David had suffered at the merciless hands of himself and his cronies were in his sobbing voice. David's spiritual reserves, which had served him so well in the past and had enabled him to suffer their many offences with an outer equanimity, were at their lowest ebb after the sadistic beating he had just suffered. His face also showed some bruising, and his legs bore the red-blue marks of the strap which Coleman had used.

Richard, filled with compassion for his awful plight, put a trembling hand on his shoulder but felt him draw away.

'I had nothing to do with such a dirty trick, or knew anything about it,' he avowed hoarsely.

'Then why did you bring me the parcel?'

'I only meant to be friendly. I swear it, Madison.'

David seemed to think for a moment and then swallowed hard.

'I'm sorry, De Macey,' he replied with a pitiful little smile. 'I believe you.'

Richard stayed with him for a few minutes commiserating with him. He would have liked to have stayed longer, but he had to see Arthur Gillespie about something. He had a plan in his mind for helping David which would require Arthur's co-opera-tion to accomplish.

19

Richard Suggests a Plan of Action

Outside the bicycle shed, Arthur Gillespie was about to teach one of the smaller pupils a lesson in psychology. The tyres of his bicycle needed pumping up, but as the afternoon was too sweltering to induce him to make the necessary effort, he asked the youngster whether he would like to do them in his stead.

'Not on your life, Arthur!' was the immediate reply, accompanied by a knowing laugh.

For a few moments Arthur observed him obliquely through his spectacles, and then, *à la* Tom Sawyer, said slowly, as he unscrewed the metal caps which secured the valves: 'I'm glad you said that.'

'What do you mean?' asked the other suspiciously, fearing some sort of trick.

'These particular tyres are specially made, and when the bike was bought I was told always to pump them up myself. It's tricky to get it right, you see. So I'm glad that you don't want to have a go, really.' The pump was now in his hands.

'I bet I could pump them up, Arthur.'

Arthur shook his head.

'I don't think so. You have to know exactly when they're just hard enough, but not *too* hard.' He screwed the connection of the pump on to one of the valves.

'Let me have a try,' begged the other. 'I won't do any damage. You can watch me to make sure.'

'Oh, all right,' said Arthur with seeming reluctance, 'I'll feel them for you and tell you when to stop.'

With much puffing and blowing, and with cheeks afire with exertion, the little goat pumped away furiously.

'There!' he exclaimed proudly when he had finished, wiping the sweat off his forehead. Arthur could contain himself no longer and burst out into a series of hoarse laughs. The truth of the ruse suddenly dawned on the sweated labourer.

'You've made a fool of me, Arthur,' he complained indignantly, accusing the amused and laughing trickster.

'You've made one of yourself,' Arthur told him in correction, shaking his head with mock gravity. 'You should be grateful to me for teaching you a valuable lesson. When you want something, make sure you really want it and not because you think you can't have it.'

With an expression of injured pride on his small countenance, the duped one strutted off.

Richard De Macey came over to the bicycle shed just after the younger pupil had left. He wasn't yet on speaking terms with Arthur and didn't quite know how to broach his plan for helping David.

'May I speak with you, Gillespie?' he asked in embarrassment, his colour heightening.

'Yes, if you want to.'

'Something will have to be done about Coleman.'

'You know my treatment – a double dose of castor oil. But what's it to you? He'd never dare lay a finger on your inviolate hide.'

Richard blushed to the roots of his hair. He resented the remark but refrained from making an angry retort.

'I know you don't like me, but it's not on account of myself. It's about Madison. Coleman gave him another brutal beating a short while ago, and he's covered with strap marks.'

'The beast! I'm with you, De Macey. Have you got any ideas?'

'If you were to ask your father to have a look at David, he'd know what to do.'

'That's a smashing plan! I should have thought of that myself ages ago. Does David know?'

'No. I don't think he'd let us do anything if he did.'

'Good! But I'll have to cycle home like the wind to catch my father before he goes off for some of his distant visits. Otherwise, he won't be back until late tonight. I'll see you later. Cheerio!'

'All right! Goodbye!'

Arthur jumped on his bicycle, but paused for an instant before setting off. 'I'm sorry for what I said to you just now.' He then went flying down the drive pedalling furiously and scattering his fellow pupils like crows before a dog. A boy or two became entangled in his wheels, but he reached the open road without serious mishap and disappeared in the direction of his home in a cloud of dust.

20

David Runs Away from School

David was feeling much better because Richard's consoling words had cheered him up. He got off the bed a few minutes after the other had left, pulled up his stockings to hide the strap marks on his legs, washed his face to remove the tear marks and, finally, combed his tousled hair. What he had resolved to do would necessitate giving the impression that he was a normal boy going on a normal journey. He had, in fact, decided to run away from St Donat's. He had weighed up the pros and cons carefully and had come to the conclusion that that was the only course left for him to take; besides saving him further misery, it would spare him the humiliation of a formal expulsion. He counted his money and searched about in his wardrobe for truant coins – in all, he had about fifteen pounds, for he had put something by each week in case he should fancy something particular someday. He had intended to use some of the money on the annual school outing in a fortnight's time – which, despite his uncertain future, he had been looking forward to – but now his nest egg was to be put to a grimmer use. He gathered a few articles of clothing together and put them in a small suitcase. It would be both convenient and strategic to travel light. On account of leaving most of his belongings behind, he probably wouldn't be missed before bedtime, when, with luck, he would be well on his way to London; and once there, he would be safe from any pursuers until he could continue on to Liverpool. He smoothed his bed where he had been lying on it. As he was on the point of going out of the dormitory, he stopped and took his red blazer out of the wardrobe with the intention of bringing it with him. He had loved that blazer once, and even now it cast a certain spell, but after a moment's hesitation he flung it away from him as if it were something unclean. He wanted no reminders of St Donat's once he had left it. To cover his tracks further, he went down to the study and put his books away neatly, for he had always done this when prep was finished for the day. He was feeling much happier as the minutes passed, and he was becoming more and more convinced that his decision was the right one – indeed, the only one. He surveyed the study for the last time with emotional eyes and then descended the stairs.

He made sure to avoid his friends. Fortunately, most of them were out playing tennis or cricket, and he reached the fields at the back of the Abbey without being seen. Two men in shirt-sleeves were mending a fence, but they paid no attention to him. He had decided that to go by road would be too dangerous; quite apart from meeting one of his friends, he might run into Coleman, or even Dr Princeton, and that was a sobering thought! Since he couldn't risk being spotted in Abbeymead by somebody who knew him, there was nothing else for it but to wait for a few hours until it was starting to get dark before attempting this hazardous part of his journey, so he sat down on a grassy bank. In his haste, he hadn't considered this delaying factor, but he was sure that he could still catch a late-night train to Liverpool from London.

The Abbey clock struck nine. It was time to resume his journey. He trotted across fields heavy with the fragrance of wildflowers, some of which were closing their petals to turn in for the night. Over fence and briar he skimmed, his knees showing little points of bleeding that were caused by nature's protective prickles. He stopped down a lane where a gaily painted Gypsy caravan was parked. Two horses were cropping the grass nearby, one a piebald, the other a chestnut with a very ancient face and a diamond-shaped blaze between its eyes. They stopped grazing to inspect him questioningly but, sensing that he intended them no harm, continued with their evening meal. Three children, the eldest of whom was about his own age, came racing down another lane in hot pursuit of one another. They were handsome youngsters, with jet-black, curly hair, dark, olive complexions, and gleaming white teeth. Colourfully embroidered jackets and pants covered their lively bodies. They regarded him interestedly with brown, flashing eyes. A woman came out of the caravan and began to stir a big iron cauldron which was suspended from a tripod over a wood fire. Like merry elves, the three children danced around the fire, while their mother stirred busily away, laughing and addressing her offspring in a strange tongue. But David could not stay to watch. The children stopped for a moment to wave at him, and he waved back.

Breaking into a trot, he entered the fields again. As he was crossing a stile, he looked back. Away in the distance the towers and roofs of St Donat's rose majestically above the surrounding trees, dominated by the spire of the church and the massive clock tower with its great clock. In spite of his lost affection for the Abbey, his heart was filled with a sudden ache for something that he had lost for ever, and a tear came into his eye. Checking a sob, he jumped down from the stile. With a cry of pain he went sprawling on the sweet-smelling grass, his suitcase flying open and spilling its contents around him.

Crawling on all fours, he collected his belongings and repacked them, and then stood up gingerly to test his foot. He discovered, with a groan, that he had twisted his ankle, not badly but enough to make the going tougher. Gritting his teeth, he limped on towards Abbeymead. A striking clock told him that he was making bad time. Coming to the first houses, he decided to take the shortest route by going through the main thoroughfare in order to compensate for lost time instead of detouring more safely by way of the backstreets. He looked up the street. Not a soul was in sight. Hurrying as much as possible, he hobbled past the shops. He hid in a doorway as a group of men came out of a public house further on, and waited until they had dispersed and gone out of sight. Assuring himself that the street was empty again, he continued on. He was just passing the pub, when he ran headlong into a customer who was just coming out. The impact caused his teeth to snap together like the jaws of a trap, and he was so shaken that he dropped his case.

'I beg your …' he began, but he was given no time to excuse himself.

'What are you doing out of bounds at this hour, Madison?' a familiar, but dreaded, voice demanded harshly. With a gasp of horror, David realized that his questioner and captor was Coleman, who, as soon as he had recognized him, had taken firm hold of him.

'Let me go!' David cried, struggling to free himself, but his captor held him firmly and delivered a few cuffs on the side of his head to subdue him.

Stooping, Coleman opened the case with one hand while keeping a firm grip on his captive with the other. The presence in it of a pair of pyjamas revealed the position. 'I see. You're running away from school, you little scoundrel. Dr Princeton will have something to say about that when we get back to the Abbey, my fine fellow.' There was no mistaking the note of anticipatory pleasure in his voice.

David renewed his efforts to escape, but he was cuffed more severely until he desisted.

'I'm not going back,' he panted, 'and you can't make me.'

'We'll see about that,' scoffed Coleman, dealing him another blow. He then began hustling him along the street despite his vigorous protests.

A young man and woman came out of the pub, and the former took a pipe out of his mouth to speak to the master.

'Goodnight, Mr Coleman!' Looking at the struggling boy, he added lightly: 'Give the little beggar a few cuffs for me while you're at it.' The woman laughed, flattering her companion's ego that he was something of a wit.

'Goodnight!' Coleman answered, raising his hat courteously to the lady.

Arm in arm, the young couple left them and crossed the street.

'He's a bit rough on the boy, isn't he?' David heard the woman say, as she leant her head on her escort's shoulder.

'Nonsense, darling,' her boyfriend replied with an air of assurance, 'boys of that age are like little brutes and have no feelings.' He took a deep, pleasurable pull of his pipe and brushed some ashes off his coat with well-manicured fingers. 'Beat them as much as you like and they won't be the worse for wear. Punishment only serves to make men out of the perishing little beggars.'

Striding down the darkening street was a Gypsy – probably from the caravan which David had seen in the lane near the village. He was tall and well built, with the same dark eyes, olive complexion and gleaming white teeth as the children. Bearded and moustached, he wore a spotted kerchief on his head, and his jacket and breeches were embroidered, just like the clothes which the youngsters had been wearing. His stride was free and majestic, and he had the bearing of a king.

'See that johnny,' the young man continued vapidly, pointing in the Gypsy's direction with the stem of his pipe. 'He's just a brute like that little tyke, only a bigger one. He's completely uncivilized, with no finer feelings, whatsoever, and as ignorant as a fool. Don't waste your sympathy on the wrong people, darling. Coleman's a decent chap and plays a good game of golf. In fact, he's probably too soft on the little perishers at the Abbey. Boys only understand the mailed fist.' With a laugh, he made a fist, and then resumed his empty-headed prattle about people from the cradle to the grave.

Meanwhile, David was being propelled unwillingly along the street, and soon the village was far behind them. When he could see the lights of the school twinkling in the distance, he made one last desperate effort to escape from his captor. He succeeded in breaking away and, despite the handicap of a sprained ankle, he covered quite a remarkable distance before Coleman caught up with him and took him into custody again. This attempt to get away angered the master, who, up to now, had been in fairly good spirits as he contemplated the fate that lay in store for his prisoner. Feeling perfectly safe from observation, as the road was deserted, Coleman dealt a few brutal blows to David's body, and David fell panting to the ground. Should Dr Princeton remark upon the bruises on the boy's face, they could easily be accounted for as having been inflicted accidentally due to his unruly behaviour after seizure, and the runaway had obligingly concealed the strap marks on his legs with his stockings.

A man peered over the nearby hedge. It was the Gypsy. He had heard the victim's distressed protests, and he took in the situation at a glance. With a thunderous expression on his face, he pushed through the hedge. He caught hold of Coleman, whose hand was again uplifted to strike his victim, and sent him sprawling into the ditch. Eyes wide with wonder, David recognized the Gypsy as the apparition which he had seen in Cloister Court on the night of Tony's emergency. There was no mistaking him, and what he had taken for a hood or cowl that night was the spotted kerchief, the rest of his colourful Romany garb exciting his overwrought imagination to see what he expected to see.

The master, in a frenzy of rage, climbed out of the ditch and rushed at the Gypsy. The two joined in battle and, after a ten-minute engagement in which Coleman fought like a madman as he sought to match the craft of his antagonist, whose telling, well-aimed blows carried the weight of fourteen stone behind them, he fell whipped and cowed on the verge of the road, his insane fury spent. With strong, white teeth showing in a friendly smile, the Gypsy lifted David to his feet; for the latter had been sitting on the ground witnessing the fight with a look of hero worship in his eyes. Bending down on one knee to bring himself down to the boy's height, the Gypsy put his hands on his shoulders and examined his face intently. David felt very secure in his champion's comforting presence. After being prompted by the other, he told his story and ended by telling of his decision to run away from school.

'No, Daveed,' said Béla – for that was the Gypsy's name – in a melodious, foreign accent. 'If you go home, your parenz will be sad. I will bring you back to St Donat'z. Yez?'

David shook his head resolutely.

'No, Béla, I don't want to go back. I'd only run away again.'

'Tomorrow, think again, and then maybe you go home, eh?'

'I can't go back. I just can't.'

Béla followed the course of a tear on his cheek with a finger and obliterated it.

'There's always some reason for things, and you are not yet – how you say it? – exbelled. Sometimes, Daveed, when trouble comes hard, we only think here' – he tapped his breast to signify the heart and its emotions – 'but up there' – he pointed towards the stars – 'God thinks here and here.' He tapped his breast and then his forehead to signify reason. 'Tomorrow, who knows, we may know what God has thought and see His reason for the pain we had yesterday.' Béla smiled at him. 'You come back now, eh, Daveed?'

'Yes, Béla,' David replied in gentle submission.

The Gypsy stood up and, towering over him, took him by the hand. He answered David's innumerable questions about himself and his life and his family – the woman and three children he had seen earlier – and he explained that, when David had mistaken him for a ghost that stormy night, he had just come from visiting Dr Princeton, who was somewhat of an authority on the Romany way of life – their discussion had been so absorbing that it was midnight before it was finished. Béla had travelled all over Europe, and he was able to speak Hungarian, Polish, French and Spanish with the same fluency as he spoke English. He had seen everything and had done everything. He could wrestle, fight with a knife or whip, mend pots, bring down fevers, tell fortunes, dress wounds, sing and play the guitar and accordion, and when necessary, chastise his merry and mischievous little children when the rascals deserved it.

David asked him whether he would ever change his way of life and settle permanently in one place instead of wandering from country to country.

'No, Daveed,' he replied. 'My home is the whole of Europe. The fields and green valleys are my garden, and the white road that turns and tweests up hill and down dale my garden path. The sky above is my roof, and the moon and stars my lanterns. You look puzzled, Daveed?'

'But what do you do when the clouds cover the moon and the stars, Béla?' asked David.

The Gypsy laughed.

'I know that God has drawn the curtains and I am content until He draws them back again. This is God's world, Daveed, so when He does a thing it must be right, and I don't ask questions why.'

David looked up at him in admiration. The breathtaking way in which he had referred to Europe, as if he could go from country to country in a single bound, captured his imagination. His answers always took proper cognizance of his Creator, so that no matter what happened in his life he was satisfied that there was a good reason for it, a reason which the morrow sometimes revealed.

David's questions were becoming less frequent now for they were nearing the Abbey, and they ceased altogether when the gates came into view. He regretted having allowed Béla to change his mind about running away, but it was too late to do anything about it now. The die was cast.

21

Richard Sounds the Alarm

In the evening, Richard and Arthur met again. Unfortunately, Dr Gillespie had left on his visit to his distant patients before Arthur arrived home, so, for the moment, their plan to help David had to remain in abeyance. They then went to look for David but could find him nowhere; but, as he had disappeared temporarily once or twice before after Coleman had punished him, they thought nothing further about it. However, as the evening wore on, and there was still no sign of him, they became a little anxious, and Richard said that if he wasn't back in the Abbey in another hour he'd go to the Headmaster and explain what had happened that afternoon. Arthur endorsed this change of plan and then cycled home for the night.

Just before bedtime Richard went up to the dormitory for a final look, in case David had slipped upstairs without him seeing him, and noticed his blazer lying on the floor. He opened David's wardrobe to put it away and discovered that there were several items of clothing missing, and, more important still, that his small suitcase was gone. He pulled down the coverlet of the bed to see if his pyjamas were still there, and, when he discovered that these, too, were gone, the truth suddenly dawned upon him. Setting his lips in determination, and somehow managing to screw his courage to the sticking-place, as Lady Macbeth says, he decided to report the matter to the Headmaster immediately.

Dr Princeton was in his study going through a pile of exercise books which belonged to the boys of Coleman's class. He was very grave in his manner and his lips were set in a thin line. That morning he had received a very disquieting letter from Lord Masefield concerning the conduct of one of his masters. Lord Masefield wrote that his son had told him about Coleman's vicious treatment of David, and that, while he was aware of the tendency of boys to exaggerate, he nevertheless had confidence in the truth of his son's story.

The Headmaster had other grounds for disquiet, too. His master's particularly offensive nickname had recently come to his knowledge and was causing him a certain amount of concern, because, by no stretch of the imagination, could he detect a vestige of affection in it. And now he was stunned by his perusal of the exercise books, for slowly the evidence was accumulating of Coleman's savage persecution of the younger pupils, with David Madison as a sort of focal point for his sadistic bent. He inspected his visitor over the rim of his reading glasses.

'Well, De Macey, do you wish to see me?'

'Yes, sir,' replied Richard, clearing his throat.

'Is it that urgent? I'm extremely busy at the moment.'

In spite of feeling distinctly uncomfortable in the Headmaster's presence, Richard took the plunge boldly.

'Yes, sir. David Madison has run away from school.'

'What's that you say?' exclaimed the Doctor, coming to his feet in alarm. 'Is this some kind of prank, De Macey?'

'No, sir.'

'But why should you conclude that he has taken such a drastic step? It is late, but he may only be out of bounds.'

'I don't think so, sir. Some of his clothes are missing from the dormitory, as well as a small suitcase which was there last night.'

'But why today of all days, De Macey? I am now in possession of some very disturbing information about what has been going on in Lower School. It was my intention to investigate in the course of the next few days, but I hadn't bargained for this catastrophe.' He sat down limply, his face showing how greatly the whole set of circumstances was affecting him.

'He was flogged this afternoon by the Bea… by Mr Coleman for something he didn't do.'

'What time was this?'

'About three o'clock, sir. Arthur Gillespie and I decided to ask his father to see him, but he had left on visits to some of his patients. I didn't see Madison again, and when I went up to the dormitory a few minutes ago to see whether he was there, I discovered that some of his things were missing.'

'How long has he been gone?'

'About five or six hours, sir.'

'This is calamitous,' the Headmaster cried. 'He is much too young to be travelling unaccompanied, and I'll never forgive myself if anything happens to him. Has Mr Coleman ever punished him like that before?'

'Yes, sir, many times. He was always picking on him at the least excuse, and treating him as if he were a troublemaker and shouldn't be in the school.'

Dr Princeton was aghast at this unvarnished statement, which served to confirm the allegations made by Tony Masefield to his father.

'Are you a friend of Madison's?'

Richard, remembering his past offences against him, blushed guiltily but manfully gave an honest answer.

'I am now, sir, but until recently I didn't like him.'

'Am I to take it, then, that I have been completely misinformed about him – about his conduct and progress, I mean?'

'Yes, sir. He is easily the best in class, but the Bea… Mr Coleman never gave him a chance. With Mr Ledwidge it was different. He treated us according to our deserts.' Richard blushed again.

'I should have suspected that something was terribly amiss when the trouble began only after Mr Ledwidge had left. But some good has come out of it. I'd say that this whole sordid business has changed you, De Macey.' The Headmaster looked inquiringly at him.

'Yes, sir,' answered Richard, meeting his gaze unwaveringly.

'Your father will be proud of you when he hears.'

'Thank you, sir.'

The Headmaster phoned the bus and railway stations in Abbeymead, but received negative answers, for neither place had seen the missing boy. He notified the police and gave them David's description. He then went out into the grounds while he waited for any news that might be forthcoming. Richard asked for permission to stay up, and this was granted. The Headmaster sent him back to Abbot's for his overcoat and cap, for it was now quite chilly, and when he returned, he told him to stay with him.

They were walking slowly down the drive when Richard pointed excitedly towards the road where three dim figures could be seen approaching. It was the Gypsy, Béla, and David, who was holding his hand, and following slowly behind, at a safe distance, was Coleman.

'Thank God he's safe!' murmured the Headmaster, with a sigh of relief, going to meet them. Coleman tried to engage his attention but was ignored. 'You look cold and hungry, Madison. You must be chilled to the bone.'

'I'm not hungry, sir,' answered David in a weak voice, keeping close to Béla.

'Nevertheless, a hot meal will do you good. Matron will find you something to eat. I trust that you won't try to run away again tonight?' A little smile played around the corners of his mouth as he said this, and Béla laughed.

'No, sir,' replied David, staring fixedly at the ground in order to avoid his eye.

'Good! I'll hold you responsible to see that he eats a good meal, De Macey.'

'I'll see to it, sir,' Richard answered, proud of being given such an important assignment. He smiled at David and took his case; and the two of them went up the drive to Matron's house, while Dr Princeton stayed behind talking to Béla.

Matron soon got a hot, nourishing meal ready, and David

discovered, after a few delicious mouthfuls, that he was ravenous. Richard was invited to join him and, remembering the Headmaster's instructions, heartily fulfilled his commission by giving example. They didn't see Dr Princeton again that night, and when they had finished eating, they went to Abbot's House and went straight up to the dormitory. Matron had warmed David's pyjamas for him, and they made him glow all over when he put them on. He was very, very tired and as soon as his head touched the pillow he dropped off to sleep.

22

Dr Princeton Holds an Investigation

When David woke up in the morning, the expectant faces of his friends silently demanded a report of his unusual adventure. Making no direct reference to his break for freedom, he recounted the episode as if it were merely incidental to what had happened beforehand instead of being the result of it. He delighted them with his description of the fight between the master and Béla, and gave them a detailed account of every blow.

'If that's the only good that comes of it, David, it was worth it,' an awed listener commented. 'I'd have given my right arm to see the Beast getting flattened and lying on the road.'

'Wait until Mr Coleman gets his hands on Madison, Belford,' Gilbert Roye said with a wicked laugh, 'and we'll see who else gets flattened.'

'Shut up, Roye,' Richard told him angrily, 'or you'll be the one who gets flattened.'

Roye fumed in silence, and Belford didn't dare answer his former friend's rebuke. The atmosphere in the dormitory was too hostile towards them, and after the shabby trick with the parcels they had to be careful and lie low for a while. So far, only Richard, David and Arthur knew about it, and they were afraid of the possible repercussions should knowledge of it spread.

It was a Saturday, but before breakfast word went round that there would be no classes that morning. Speculations were rife – some said that the grapevine was in error and that there would be classes as usual; others suggested that the cancellation had something to do with the unwelcome inspection of their exercise books by the Headmaster the evening before. Richard and Arthur guessed that it had to do with Coleman, for the Headmaster had asked Arthur's father to examine David, and shortly after breakfast he had done so. Their guess was confirmed, and the whole school was soon buzzing with the news that Dr Princeton was holding an investigation in order to clear up the dreadful state of affairs that had come to his attention. The Headmaster was already satisfied that what he had heard about Coleman's sadistic cruelty was true, but he felt that an open inquiry would help to restore the confidence of the younger boys in his administration of the school. A boy was sent to summon the master to his study, and when the latter came, the Headmaster curtly motioned him to sit down on the other side of his desk. Coleman had quickly guessed what was afoot after receiving the summons, and his attitude, at present, was a mixture of defiance and resentment.

'Th-this is an outrage,' he cried with as much indignation as he thought advisable under the circumstances, for as yet he was not aware how much Dr Princeton knew about things. 'Am I to be accused without so much as a hearing?'

'You'll get your chance to speak later. I might never have known anything about what's been going on if Lord Masefield hadn't written to me about certain allegations his son had made about you.' He picked up a letter that was on the table and dropped it back again. 'They concern your conduct here, with emphasis on your brutal persecution of Madison.'

'Masefield is tarred with the same brush as Madison. They were as thick as thieves together. No one would believe anything coming from their lying lips.'

'This inquiry is not so much for my benefit as for the benefit of the boys of Lower School. If not lost completely, their confidence in my administration of the school must be shaken to its core. I intend to restore as much of it as I can.'

Thornley was summoned and Dr Princeton smiled at him to put him at his ease.

'I'd like to hear your account, Thornley, of what has been going on here since Mr Ledwidge left. You may speak freely. There will be no reprisals.'

Thornley looked at Coleman and then back at the Headmaster before speaking.

'Since the Bea… Mr Coleman came, sir, life for most of us hasn't been worth living, but for David Madison it has been sheer hell. Excuse me, sir.'

'Never mind. Please go on.'

'He's borne the brunt of his brutality. For the rest of us, it has mostly been a matter of needless fault-finding and endless lines …'

'This boy has never co-operated with me,' Coleman exclaimed angrily, cutting in on the damning evidence. 'He has persistently sided with those whom I've found fit to punish. He has even dared to question my authority and methods in front of the other boys.'

Thornley looked him straight in the eye and addressed him directly.

'I offered to resign my captaincy once, but you wouldn't let me.'

'Perhaps if you had succeeded in doing so, Thornley,' observed the Headmaster, 'I might have got some inkling of the truth earlier. Since I've been at the school, no one has yet voluntarily relinquished such a position of honour.'

'Are you insinuating that I refused to allow this lying wretch to resign in case you should come to hear something you shouldn't?' Coleman demanded.

'You would never have said that unless it were uppermost in your mind.'

The other glowered impotently but said nothing.

Dr Princeton turned to the Captain. 'Tell me, Thornley, in

your opinion, has discipline improved under the present regime or not.'

'If anything, it has become worse, sir. If we were to keep all the rules and regulations that Cole... Mr Coleman insists on we wouldn't be able to breathe. Most of the fellows don't even understand half of them.'

'You imply that, with Mr Ledwidge, the school rules were interpreted liberally? Is that so?'

'Yes, sir. We didn't need policing when he was here. Except for a few chaps, we respected him too much to play on his good nature. Even doing normal things now seems to infringe some rule or other.'

'I understand,' said Dr Princeton, nodding. 'But why didn't you come to me? Did you think that I'm not sufficiently interested in the welfare of the pupils to put things right? Did you think that I would have dismissed you without a hearing and made no effort to establish the truth?'

Thornley shifted uncomfortably. It was a very awkward question to answer.

'I don't rightly know, sir. I may have thought that you would side with one of the teaching staff against us, no matter who was in the right.'

'I appreciate you frankness, Thornley. Lower School couldn't have a better or more faithful Captain. You may go now. Tell De Macey to come in.'

'Yes, sir.' After glancing at Coleman, who glared venomously back, Thornley left the study.

'The boy is spinning a wild, fictitious yarn. He is not reliable in one word he says. Am I to be given any chance to explain anything?'

'What happened yesterday afternoon?' the Headmaster asked without preamble.

'Madison stole a parcel of mine and I punished him.'

'What proof had you of his guilt?'

'I caught him red-handed when he was opening it.'

'Where?'

'In the study.'

Dr Princeton put the tips of his fingers together.

'Why did you suspect him? Surely he couldn't have been the only suspect?'

'I didn't say that he was,' grumbled the other.

'Then how did you find out?'

'Belford told me that he'd taken it.'

'Is that the whole story?'

'Of course it is. I've given you the relevant facts.'

There was a knock on the door and Richard De Macey entered.

'Did you wish to see me now, sir?'

'Yes, De Macey. Please sit down.' Richard did so. 'If you know anything that might have some bearing on yesterday's incident regarding the parcel, I'd like to hear it.'

'When I went into Abbot's House in the afternoon, sir, there was a parcel for Madison on the table, and I brought it up to him in his study.'

'Was there any particular reason for doing so?'

'I did it to be friendly, sir,' Richard replied, blushing.

'I understand. You told me about your change of attitude towards him. It *was* addressed to Madison?'

'Yes, sir.'

'Did you inspect the label, Mr Coleman?'

'I saw no reason to,' was the shifty answer. 'I had no reason to doubt Belford's word. In any case, Madison has enough cunning to have altered it in case of discovery.'

'I see. You automatically assumed that he was guilty. In other words, you considered him fair game for your sadistic bent.'

'Th-this is grossly insulting. You are drawing unwarranted conclusions.'

'Did you find out your mistake?'

'How was I to know? He had my parcel. I was misinformed.'

Richard turned to him.

'I told you that it was addressed to Madison, but you refused to listen. I also told you that I had brought it to him.'

'Does that refresh your memory?' asked the Headmaster.

'It slipped my mind. I can't remember everything I hear or do.'

'You conveniently forget what is pertinent when it doesn't suit. You've been most helpful, De Macey. Please be good enough to find Belford for me.'

'Very good, sir,' said Richard, leaving the study.

'How am I to be expected to exert authority when you treat me like a criminal in front of those in my charge?' Coleman demanded bitterly. 'Nothing could be more farcical.'

'Farce suggests something essentially humorous,' observed the Doctor grimly, 'but I fail to detect any element of humour in this distressing business.'

'You are allowing these scheming boys to vent their venom against me. They are grotesquely exaggerating the most minute details.'

'I don't doubt, for an instant, the accuracy of their statements.'

Belford came in, a frightened, uneasy, hangdog expression on his coarse face.

'Sit down, Belford. I wish to hear your version of yesterday's incident.'

'You mean about Madison, sir?' he asked guiltily.

'Yes, I mean about Madison.'

Belford swallowed hard. He was prepared to say anything to keep himself in the clear, but he was handicapped in three ways: firstly, he was too dishonest a boy to be able to appear to tell the truth; secondly, he was much too stupid to be able to stick to a consistent pattern of lies; and thirdly, he was in the dark about how much Coleman and De Macey had already told the Headmaster.

'Mr Coleman asked me about a parcel which the porter had left in the hall of Abbot's for him, sir.'

'And you informed him that there was one there?'

'That's right, sir.'

'Did you tell him anything else?'

Belford looked with uncertainty at Coleman before responding.

'No, sir,' he replied, in the hope that the Headmaster was only fishing for information and had but a mere inkling of what had really occurred.

Dr Princeton regarded him severely.

'Did you, or did you not, also tell him that Madison had taken it?'

Belford became confused. He didn't know where his answers were taking him, and his slow brain was trying fruitlessly to cope with the situation.

'I … I did, sir. I forgot to mention that.'

'I don't believe you. You're sure Madison took it?'

'Yes, I saw him.'

'It has already been established that De Macey delivered it to Madison, and that it was also addressed to him.'

'De Macey's a liar,' Belford almost shouted, 'My word's as good as his.'

'Don't raise your voice when speaking to me, Belford. I warn you not to make matters worse by attempting to defame others. There is, obviously, foul play at work in this business, and you have a lot of explaining to do to extricate yourself from having had a major part in it.'

Belford knew that the game was up and that he had completely failed to convince his questioner that what he said was true. There was only one way out, and that was to put the blame on someone else. He had had a lesson in that stratagem from Gilbert Roye the day before, when the latter had tried to blame him when Richard had discovered their dirty plot; and he was now about to show that he was no slow learner – at least, where skulduggery was concerned. He also had this advantage – Roye had yet to tell *his* story.

'It was all Gilbert Roye's fault, sir. I wanted nothing to do with it, and I tried to stop him.'

'Go on, Belford, I'm listening,' said the Headmaster, looking sternly at him.

Belford licked dry lips.

'There were two parcels. One was for Mr Coleman and the other for Madison. Roye swapped the labels to get Madison into trouble. I didn't want to do it, but I was bullied into it.'

'I see it all clearly now. You are one of the most despicable boys I have ever encountered in a long teaching career. You may go now, but you have not heard the last of this.' Belford slunk out of the study like a man on his way to the gallows.

Gilbert Roye was called in next, and, after him, several other boys of Abbot's House. They all came into the study anxiously, hesitantly, not relishing the prospect of being interrogated by the Headmaster – and Coleman's presence was enough to make even the bravest heart quail.

Dr Princeton put each one on his honour to speak the truth or else remain silent, and, except for the pusillanimous few, the boys bravely sweated it out. Not one of these gave precedence to his own sufferings under the regime, but David was mentioned in almost every breath. The phone rang while the last boy was telling his story. It was Dr Gillespie. He informed the Headmaster that David was covered from head to foot with bruises, which could have been inflicted only by a vicious, sadistic beating with strap and fist.

'Well, Coleman,' Dr Princeton demanded, when the last boy whom he had been questioning had gone out, 'what have you to say for yourself now? You have been anxious to defend yourself since you came in.'

Coleman was quivering with rage and was too speechless to answer immediately.

'There's … there's a conspiracy against me,' he cried, when he had found his voice. 'No one in his right senses would accept as true a single word that's been said. The boys of Lower School are completely without a shred of decency, every last one of them. Until I came here, they were half-wild through lack of discipline. It was obvious that the decrepit old invalid who preceded me was unable to control them.'

'Are you quite finished?' asked the Doctor, with dangerous calm.

'No, I'm not. You've listened to their drivel, and I'm entitled to refute it. Who are you to interfere with kid-glove methods when what the little hooligans need is the rod and plenty of other disciplinary measures, too. Boys of their age are like brutes, without reason or feelings. If I am to be master in my own class-room …'

Dr Princeton cut him short. None of the boys had ever known him to lose his temper, but a legend was born that day to the effect that when he finally castigated Coleman every building within a hundred yards of the study trembled as he gave vent to his feelings.

'You will never darken the threshold of one of my classrooms again, and if I have anything to do with it, you will never teach again! You're not fit to be in charge of impressionable young minds. You're not even fit to be in charge of wild animals, although I doubt if your kind of courage would suit you for such an occupation.' His voice was heavy with sarcasm. 'You are beneath contempt. You vent your sadistic evil on defenceless boys and, not content with that, you concentrate most of it on the most defenceless of them all.'

Coleman was livid with fury.

'How dare you! How dare you! Madison is a little brute with indifferent upbringing and deserves treatment as such.'

'Silence! Don't attempt to interrupt me again. You talk about a conspiracy and lies, but you attribute them to the wrong source.' The Headmaster picked up a number of exercise books off the table and dropped them back one by one as he commented on them. 'I've been looking through these since yesterday, and what I've seen appals me. Roye, Belford – hopeless scholars with ridiculously high marks. Masefield – not a brilliant boy, by any means, but well above average, with shocking reports. Thornley and Gillespie – plodders both, but by no means the idiots you try to make them out to be. De Macey – here the sudden changeover from absurdly good marks, when he was in favour, to equally absurdly bad ones, when he fell out of it, is glaringly obvious – this, in spite of the fact that his later work shows increasing improvement. And Madison – here your insane venom surpasses itself. He is the most brilliant pupil who has ever come to this school, and yet you mark his work as if he were a moron. His exercise books are cut to ribbons from the vicious tracks of your pencils and insolent comments. But you were not even contented with that. Failing to break his noble spirit, you endeavoured, almost with success, to have him expelled. He is covered with the most brutally inflicted bruises, which would be sufficient evidence of your terrible treatment of him if no other were available. I do not have to mention his psychological inju-ries. You belong behind bars, and you can be prepared for the worst. I shall give my full support to whatever measures his parents think should be taken.'

'I won't allow myself to be spoken to like …'

'I have had sufficient of your bluster and cowardly defence. Get out of this room this instant. You are no longer a master here, and I expect you to be out of the school by the afternoon.'

The Headmaster's face was as grim as death, and his lips were curled with contempt. Coleman, his features satanically contorted, was about to speak again, but Dr Princeton pointed scornfully towards the door, and he slunk out of the study. Poetic justice was well served, for it was Coleman, and not David, who was being expelled from the school like a whipped cur with his tail between his legs.

Dr Princeton rested his forehead on his hands to recover some of his lost composure before he summoned the one who was the chief actor in this terrible drama. David came in hesitantly.

'Sit down, Madison,' the Headmaster told him gently. 'I just don't know what to say to you. No words of mine could ever adequately express my feelings about the dreadful outrages that have been committed against you. And the thought that a boy of your calibre might have been expelled so unjustly, and have a promising scholastic career so unjustly ended, frankly appals me.'

David could hardly believe his ears. His face brightened, and his eyes lit up.

'Then I'm not to be expelled, sir?'

'Expelled!' exclaimed the Headmaster, his voice shaking with remorse. 'Never mention that word in my hearing again, Madison! No, Madison,' he continued more quietly, 'it is I who deserve expulsion. For the past few months, when you were living under that constant threat, I failed this wonderful old school. I had the effrontery to tell you to put your house in order when it was mine that was at fault. May I hope for your forgiveness?'

David did not fully understand everything that the Headmaster was saying, but the general meaning was quite clear. His heart was full of mixed emotions due to the sudden change in his circumstances. He felt a strong desire to cry, he was so happy and relieved, but somehow he managed to keep his feelings under control.

'I have nothing to forgive you for, sir. I have never blamed you for anything. You always treated me kindly. You didn't know what was happening.'

The Headmaster was touched by his great generosity of spirit.

'Thank you, Madison. But it was my duty to know. Instead, I believed when I was told about your supposed idleness and lack of discipline. I have just had the misfortune to meet three of the most despicable persons I have ever known. I now have the good fortune to meet one of the most noble.'

'Thank you, sir.'

'Don't thank me, Madison. I have already thought the worst about you, and, now that I know the true position, the best. But it is immaterial what I think. Your nobility is a fact, and nobody can ever take that away from you by mere thinking. Don't blame

St Donat's for what has happened, but its Headmaster. You may rest assured that the like will never occur in this school again. You are rich in friends here, and I am proud of the way they've stood by you and by one another. I shall write to your parents without delay and explain everything that has happened before deciding what should be done about Coleman.'

'Please, sir, I'd rather you didn't tell them anything. It would only make them unhappy.'

'Do you mean to say that they have no inkling whatsoever of what has been going on here?' asked the Headmaster in astonishment.

'Yes, sir.'

'You brave boy! But I feel bound in duty to inform them.'

'Please, sir!' pleaded David earnestly. 'It's all over now. Please!'

'I don't know, Madison,' was the thoughtful reply. 'I feel I can't remain silent. Justice still needs to be done, but I shall do all in my power to handle the matter in a way that will be agreeable to your parents without causing you any further unnecessary pain. Will that suit you?'

'Yes, sir.'

Tears were beginning to well up in his eyes and he started fumbling for his handkerchief.

'Tears will help to wash away the memory of much of the past evil, Madison,' said the Headmaster gently.

David's emotions, pent-up for so long, suddenly overwhelmed him, and the tears deluged his eyes until the calming flood had run its course. He felt that he had just woken up after a nightmare. At least, that was the feeling, but not once during his terrible persecution had he been asleep, and his terror had been all too real then.

23

David Spends a Full Afternoon

David didn't know whether he was standing on his head or on his heels on the afternoon of that memorable day of exoneration and reinstatement; and, in spite of the appeals of his ecstatic friends to join them on a visit to Abbeymead to celebrate their liberation from the Beast's tyrannous rule, he spent the first few hours in his own way. He just rambled about the Abbey, inside and out, recapturing the old enchantment which had vanished with Coleman's arrival there. Gone was the menacing look of the buildings – no prison they, but ancient, weather-beaten, kindly old edifices which towered above him in maternal protection. The clock in the clock tower, with its four big dials which faced the four cardinal points of the compass, seemed to whisper to him on the soft breezes that it had been watching yesterday's flight in case he had come to harm, and he smiled up at it as he stood in Cloister Court. Through Great Cloister he strolled, then through Cloister Passage to the chapel where he gave thanks for his timely and almost miraculous acquittal.

Afterwards, when his friends had returned from Abbeymead, he joined them and went with them into the nearby woods. While they climbed trees and generally conducted themselves with wild abandon, he could only look on and play a verbal part in their sport because his ankle, which he had sprained the day before when running away from school, still had a weak, nagging feeling about it and prevented his active participation. When they arrived back at the school later, exhausted but in high spirits, he left them and went upstairs to the study. But not to work – the day was too signal a one for that – but just simply to enjoy a favourite place of his which had so many pleasant associations – with the unforgettable exception of the one before he ran away.

He opened the door, and there, perched on a table waiting for him, and looking none the worse for his midnight emergency, was Tony Masefield, his brown eyes shining like twin stars. It would be impossible to say whether David's pleasure at their reunion was greater than Tony's, or vice versa. They rushed towards each other in greeting, their words mixing in joyful confusion, while Arthur Gillespie, who was also in the study, sat watching them like a benign uncle.

'I would have to miss all the fun,' Tony lamented, when their delirium at their reunion had lessened. 'Why couldn't I be here when the Beast was being hauled over the coals? I'd have told the Doctor a darn sight more about him than I told my father. I came back today because I thought I'd be in time for the fire-works. Then to miss everything by a measly few hours!'

'You set the ball rolling, Tony,' Arthur reminded him.

'Still, I was nearly too late. If David had succeeded in getting as far as London, it might have been a different story. His parents would probably never have sent him back here, no matter what was done to put things right.'

David smiled happily at him.

'It's all over and done with now, Tony, so it makes no differ-ence. It was like a bad dream.'

'Prison's the only place for a brute like him, and I hope they put him there and throw away the key.'

Arthur peered knowingly over the rim of his glasses.

'It's not a prison that he needs, Tony, but an asylum. I'd say he's a mental case. That reminds me – I was told to bring David over to the house for a feed. Of course, that includes you now.'

'Did you hear that insult, David?' cried Tony facetiously. 'He would have forgotten to ask us if he hadn't associated us with mental cases.'

'I'm sure he didn't mean me, Tony. Thanks, Arthur. But we're continually being invited there, and we can't return the compliment.'

Arthur gave a hoarse laugh.

'My parents only invite you boys over to remind them how superior their own one is.'

'How is it that I can never think of anything nice to say, like David?' Tony wondered. 'Of course, I've never been noted for diplomacy.'

'How did you like the blood transfusion?' Arthur asked him.

'I was too weak to notice much. But look.' He pointed at a fresh scar on his neck. 'I've got a scar about a foot long where the surgeon incised for the abscess.'

Arthur inspected it.

'It's only a small mark, so don't exaggerate. It was probably a keyhole incision.'

'I'll let you measure it with a ruler someday. You've insulted my scars much too often. I got a lot of doctors out of their beds that night, I can tell you. The whole hospital was in an uproar.'

'You told us just now that you hadn't noticed much,' David reminded him with a laugh.

'You're as bad as Arthur at times. I wasn't weak *all* the time. The Masefields would have lost their heir apparent but for you, David.' He was serious now. 'They say I owe my life to you, and none of us will ever forget it.'

'I happened to wake up at the right moment, Tony, that's all.'

'It was more than that. Do you ever think how things fit in?'

'Yes, I do. Often.'

Tony explained for Arthur's benefit.

'If David hadn't come to St Donat's, Arthur, I'd probably have died that night, for nobody else would have noticed that there was anything wrong. And if I hadn't conked out, the Doctor wouldn't have given him another chance and he would have been expelled, and that would have put the lid on it.'

'Then there was yesterday, Tony. If your father's letter hadn't come just when it did, I might still … oh, but it's so confusing. Arthur wouldn't understand if I went on. I hardly do myself.' It was a complex sequence of events, but he could see the various connecting links. Also, he was satisfied now that he understood why God had allowed him to suffer so much. Béla, the Gypsy, had indeed been right about how important the morrow was as it sometimes revealed His reason for past events.

There was a knock on the door, and Charlie, the school porter, poked his head in. He was obviously pleased to see Tony looking so alive and well and told him so in his bluff, open-hearted way. He handed David a parcel, which, he said, he had found in the boiler room, and then went out. David had forgotten completely about the one that was supposed to have come for him, and had regarded it somewhat of a myth, as if it had never actually existed. With mounting excitement, he opened it. It was from Tony's parents and contained a beautifully bound set of reference books for young people, suitably inscribed on the front page of the first volume with their thanks.

'How do you like them, David?' asked Tony, enjoying his delight at getting them.

'They're beautiful, Tony. I must write to your parents over the weekend and thank them. They must have been jolly expensive.'

'They wouldn't dream of sending anything but the best to you.'

'It's strange,' murmured Arthur, more to himself than to his friends, 'that this happened to be the parcel that brought everything to a head, but in the end put everything right.'

But it didn't seem so strange to his two friends, and Tony and David smiled at each other at this further indication that their lives were somehow connected more than could be accounted for by mere coincidence. Thornley dropped into the study later, followed by a very embarrassed De Macey; and while he assured himself that Tony was in good shape by feeling his muscles and prodding him in the chest, Richard made a few blushing inquiries about his health. Tony had already heard about Richard's part in the climax of events and, mindful of the night when he had testified to his courage, was as friendly with him as if that was the way it had always been.

'I can hardly believe that the Beast's been sent packing in disgrace,' Thornley said when he had finished examining Tony, 'and I don't suppose I'll really believe it until I actually see his successor.'

'You're a doubting Thomas,' Tony told him. 'Anyway, we can rely on the Doctor to see that we don't get another Coleman'.

'I always said that Dr Princeton was a headmaster in a million,' Arthur commented, 'and he's certainly proved it. He told my father that he was very proud of the way the Lower School boys had stood together.'

'Tell us another one, Arthur,' said the Captain disbelievingly.

'There he goes doubting again,' Tony said, clicking his tongue. 'What's to be done with him?'

David laughed.

'I've told him the same thing, so perhaps he'll believe it now.'

'And he mentioned you in particular, Thornley,' Arthur chimed in.

'You're fibbing, Arthur?'

'No, I'm not. I'd swear it on my honour.'

'I certainly believe it,' David said in corroboration. 'You never let us down once, and you couldn't have been in a more awkward position.'

The Captain lowered his head modestly.

'I did my best. But you're the real hero, David. You put the kibosh on the brute.'

'I'm not going to tell you what the Doctor said about David,' Arthur said, chuckling hoarsely. 'I want to spare his blushes.'

'Thornley will always get my vote for Captain,' David interposed quickly in case Arthur had second thoughts about the matter and decide to tell them anyway.

'Mine, too,' Tony promised. 'He's a brick.'

Thornley smiled at him and winked at the others.

'I remember you telling me once that I'd never get your vote for Captain again.'

'You shouldn't believe all I say. You stuck to us like glue through thick and thin. Why are you so silent, Richard? You've hardly uttered a word.'

'I wasn't of much help.' He was feeling very much an outsider because of his previous behaviour and because of the nature of the conversation.

'You made up for everything in the end, Richard,' Thornley assured him. 'You played your part at just the right moments.'

'Thanks, Thornley. David!'

'Yes, Richard?'

'I said once that the day would never come when I'd apologize to you because of the way I treated you; but, before your friends, I apologize now and hope you will forgive me. I was nothing but a prig and unbearable snob.' He was now very embarrassed and tried desperately to hide how he was feeling. His listeners greatly admired his gesture in making his apology so publicly. David accepted it graciously, and he was surprised how easy it had been, after all.

'Roye and Belford are being taken away from the school,' De Macey informed them, less ill at ease now that the apology was off his chest. 'Dr Princeton phoned their parents and told them that he couldn't be responsible for what might happen to them if they were to stay on here.'

'The Doctor understands boys,' exclaimed Tony with sudden belligerence, 'because if I had got my hands on them …'

'Take it easy, Tony,' Thornley advised, laughing. 'We don't want you to burst another blood vessel. I almost forgot to tell you more good news. We've won the rugger cup. Our opponents can't field a team against us in the final.'

'They must have heard that I was back.'

'That's great news!' exclaimed Arthur. 'All the hard knocks we took this season were worth it. We can rest on our laurels now for a while.'

Richard smiled at him.

'I'm afraid I must disappoint you, Arthur. Thornley has drawn up extra training sessions for the cricket.'

'We can concentrate on that now,' the Captain told them. 'Something tells me that this is going to be St Donat's year for sport.'

'Coleman nearly finished our chances in the Cup. It's a good job we had the right skipper.'

'Somehow, Richard, I think that his efforts at sabotage made us more determined to win just to spite him.'

Later on, after Thornley and Richard had left them, David went with his two friends over to Arthur's house for the promised meal. He was ecstatically happy. And never again would he be afraid because of the alleged haunting of the Abbey. In his mind, Béla and the Abbot were so closely identified with each other that he was quite sure that the spectre would do him no harm, or cause him the slightest apprehension, should it ever show up.

24

The Return of Cincinnatus

The boys were in their classroom early on Monday morning.
There was much excitement in the air – and not a little apprehension – for no one had yet seen the master who would be
taking Coleman's place. Expectant eyes kept watching the door,
and everyone was on his best behaviour.

'I'm glad to see how spruced up you all are,' Thornley
observed approvingly as he reviewed them. 'We must make a
good impression on him when he comes. First impressions
matter.'

'Have you seen him yet?' inquired one of the backbenchers.

'I tried to yesterday, but he had gone out. I've got a little
speech of welcome ready for him.'

'Is it the same one that you had for the Beast?' Tony Masefield
asked innocently. 'You know, the one you never delivered.'

The Captain's answer was drowned in the merry outburst of
laughter at this reminder. Almost everyone had something to say
in order to shut out the nagging fear that, despite their high
expectations, they might only find themselves out of the frying
pan and into the fire. There were more doubting Thomases in
the class than Tony would have thought possible. David was just
as excited as the others, and like them, too, he also was a little
fearful that Coleman would come through the door to wreak
vengeance upon them because of what had happened. At last,
keen ears detected footsteps coming down the corridor, and with
bated breaths the boys watched the door open.

It couldn't be, but it was. With expressions of relief and delight on their faces, they mentally wiped beads of sweat off their foreheads. David's shining eyes followed Mr Ledwidge as he walked to the table, no movement being too small to pass unnoticed. The old master was more erect in posture than he had been before he went on sick leave, and there was more of a spring in his step. He was also looking well and had put on weight.

After the first shock of joyful surprise had passed, the class came hurriedly to its feet.

Mr Ledwidge beamed at them.

'Why are you staring, boys? You'd think I was a ghost or something. I hope I'm not too much of a surprise for you.' He had not intended to take up duty again until after the summer holidays but, on hearing of the horrendous happenings since his departure, he had cut his convalescence short and returned to the Abbey the day before. Like Cincinnatus of old, he came when he thought he was needed. 'You needn't try to impress me,' he added, shaking his wise old head. 'I am too well acquainted with the lot of you – whited little sepulchres who can't translate the Classics.' The boys laughed delightedly. It was apparent that his illness hadn't affected his quiet sense of humour which they enjoyed so much. 'I've heard about our continuing success in our sporting fixtures, Thornley. You are to be congratulated for doing an excellent job against stiff odds. I trust you will remain Captain for many years to come.'

There was a spontaneous chorus of 'Hear! Hear!' from the boys, and Thornley lowered his head modestly.

'As long as the boys will have me, sir.'

'Good! I've had a good report from the Headmaster about you, De Macey, and I shall be able to give your father a very gratifying account about you this year.'

'Thank you, sir,' answered Richard, smiling.

'We'll have to put our backs into our Latin more strongly, in future, won't we, Gillespie?'

Arthur chuckled hoarsely.

'I'll do my best, sir.'

'Well, Masefield? I see that you've fully recovered from *your* illness, too.'

'Yes, sir,' answered Tony proudly. 'I'm as fit as a fiddle now – but I nearly died.'

Mr Ledwidge hid a smile.

'You mustn't frighten us like that again.'

'I'll try not to, sir.'

The master next rested his kindly gaze on David, who, like all the others, was enjoying his remarks immensely.

'What can I say about you, Madison? I believe that you've had a very stormy passage during my absence,'

'It was a bit rough all right, sir,' David admitted, pleased at this show of interest in his past plight.

'However, the storm is over now, with calm waters ahead. Why are you sitting in the front row? I recall seeing your face at the back near the window.' Mr Ledwidge guessed the reason, but he wanted to rehabilitate his pupil – if that were still needed – in every way he could.

'I was put here by the last master, sir.'

Mr Ledwidge looked at him in mock severity.

'Are you questioning my authority in my own classroom, Madison?'

'No, sir.'

'Then please return to your usual seat. To the old, changes are very distracting.'

'Now, sir?'

'This very minute. Perhaps some of your knowledge may rub off on those two old soldiers, Masefield and Gillespie.'

With happiness written in every movement, David gathered up his books and was soon installed between his two friends, who were both as delighted as he was himself. It seemed years since they had sat side by side.

'Are you satisfied now that you're back among the chaff?' asked the old man, smiling, when he was seated.

'Yes, sir.'

Thornley gave him a nudge and whispered something to him. 'We're glad to see you back, sir,' he said shyly, acting as spokesman for the Captain and the rest of the class.

'And I'm glad to be back, Madison.'

'You're looking well, sir.'

'Thank you! I'm feeling well, too. Freed from the responsibility of this class of young reprobates, I've put on a stone in weight since I saw you all last.'

'That's good to hear, sir.'

Mr Ledwidge regarded him kindly.

'We've both had a stormy passage, Madison, but nevertheless we've both won through with flying colours, and in the long run, that's what really counts.'

David, his eyes aglow with happiness, smiled at him. During the lesson that followed, he hardly knew what was going on, for he was almost in a state of bliss. He thought about the last few momentous days: on Friday, he had tried to run away from the Abbey, his whole world having collapsed about him; the following day, Coleman, the brutal tyrant and his merciless oppressor, had been ignominiously dismissed by the Headmaster; Tony had returned to school; and now, Mr Ledwidge, his much respected and so loved master, was back. Everything was back to glorious normality. He could ask for nothing more.

25

Richard Reaps a Rich Harvest

Once he had abandoned his old associates and was free of them for good, Richard De Macey set about seeking more suitable friends and had soon reaped many valuable friendships. With Roye and Belford gone, the remainder of the old outcast group broke up, and its members, wisely deciding that there was safety in numbers, merged as inconspicuously as they could into more healthy society. During the following weeks Richard, whenever he got the chance, had friendly, if still quite formal, chats with David. He craved a special relationship with him because he now realized that there were few boys who could ever hope to become his equal in character, and he envied Tony and Arthur because of their pre-eminent place in his affections. So far, however, he was making little headway. He guessed that David would also like their relations to be on a warmer basis, but it was up to himself to take the initiative – David was too reserved by nature to make the first move. At least, so he reasoned. He was like a boy who wishes to mend a broken relationship but hesitates to do anything about it in case he should suffer a humiliating rebuff.

David saw Béla several times afterwards and learned a lot more about the Romany way of life. One evening, when he was coming back from the village with Tony and Arthur, he saw the Gypsy's caravan, drawn by the horse with the ancient face and diamond-shaped blaze between its eyes, emerging slowly from a lane a few hundred yards ahead.

'Béla! Béla!' he cried at the top of his voice.

The caravan lurched to a halt. Béla stood up in the driver's seat and waved, and his wife's head appeared over the half-door surrounded by a collar of waving children.

'*Adios*, Daveed!' he cried in farewell in his melodious, foreign voice.

'*Adios*, Béla!' David yelled back.

He stood watching and waving until the other's painted home had gone rolling down a side road. Béla would never lose a special niche in David's heart, for he had been his saviour and a tower of strength in his hour of greatest need, and of the utmost influence in getting him to see things from a less depressing perspective.

The boys continued on their way back to the school. When they got there, Arthur took his bike out of the bicycle shed and David got on it for a ride.

'Let's see how fast you can go, David!' Tony urged with a laugh.

David shot off down the drive, standing on the pedals in order to get more driving power. As he was coming back towards them on the return journey up the drive, one of his shoelaces became entangled in the chain. The bike jerked to a stop and bucked like a horse, and David was thrown over the handlebars. Arthur and Tony, anxious in case he had hurt himself, ran over to him; and they were joined by Richard De Macey, who was on his way to the playing fields with his cricket bat over his shoulder. They helped him up off the ground, but when he tried to stand his left leg gave under him, and a look of agony flitted across his face.

'It's my ankle – the same one I sprained before,' he told them, with a grimace, putting all of his weight on the other leg. 'It hurts much more now, though. I hope it'll be all right for Cambridge.' He was referring to the school outing there which was taking place in a few days' time and which he was looking forward to with great anticipation.

The ankle was swelling and looked bruised, so Arthur loosened his shoelace and it felt more comfortable.

'Matron will strap it for you, David, and my father will take a look at it when he comes over later – just in case. But don't put your weight on it until he sees it. You might do more damage.'

'I'll help him over to Matron, if you like,' Richard volunteered, blushing, thinking this an excellent opportunity for fostering more cordial relations with the casualty and trying desperately to hide his bat.

'It's all right, Richard,' Arthur said. 'We can manage. In any case, we wouldn't want you to lose any practice. Would we, David?'

'No, Arthur. But thanks, anyway, Richard.' David smiled at him in recompense for his offer, and then went hobbling towards the main entrance of the school with an arm around each of his friends for support.

A blush still lingered on Richard's cheek as he strolled over to the cricket ground; he felt that perhaps he had shown too much eagerness to help. At the same time, however, he would have given his right arm to have been accepted as an ambulance-man. David and he were just as formal with each other as ever.

On the eve of the outing to Cambridge, he learned that Dr Gillespie had forbidden David to go on account of the severity of the sprain. The doctor realized that high jinks would be the order of the day and was afraid that his young patient might reinjure the ankle in trying to keep pace with his friends. After vacillating for some time, Richard decided on a bold manoeuvre, which entailed, as a kick-off, going to see the Headmaster.

'What can I do for you, De Macey?' Dr Princeton asked, putting the tips of his fingers together and inspecting him from head to foot, although Richard suspected that the pose was more from habit than from any intention to intimidate.

'It's about David Madison, sir,' Richard said in embarrassment, shifting his weight from one foot to the other and half wishing that he hadn't been quite so daring in the first place.

Dr Princeton raised his eyebrows inquiringly. 'Madison?'

'Yes, sir. He sprained his ankle the other day and Dr Gillespie has forbidden him to go to Cambridge tomorrow.'

'I see. Well?'

'May I have your permission, sir, to ask Dr Gillespie's permission to permit him to go with me instead to the Norfolk Broads if I can get my aunt's permission to use her car and chauffeur?' Richard knew that he had put his request very badly.

'That's a very complicated request, De Macey,' commented the Headmaster, with only the suspicion of a smile on his lips. 'Am I right in supposing that you wish me to allow you to ask Dr Gillespie to allow Madison to go with you to the Norfolk Broads if your aunt allows you the use of her car and driver?'

'Yes, sir.' Richard was glad that even the Headmaster found it difficult to express his petition less awkwardly, or at least wanted to spare him further embarrassment by not endeavouring to do so.

'You are to be congratulated for fathering such a very fine thought, De Macey – despite its convolutions. If you had asked me this a month or so ago, I would have refused you out of hand. But since then you have shown what I can only describe as a miraculous improvement in your whole attitude, both towards life in general and towards your studies. I don't see how I can refuse your request. You have earned it.'

'Thank you, sir.'

As he was leaving the study, the Headmaster called after him.

'Yes, sir?'

'I hope you're successful, De Macey.'

'Thank you, sir.'

He next went to see his aunt who lived with a lady-companion in a rambling country house a few miles from the Abbey. She was a partially deaf old lady and was continually experimenting with new hearing aids, apparently expecting to get twice as good hearing as a normal person with some instrument which she had still to find. When he arrived, she was preparing to test a fresh batch of models that had just been delivered. Richard was a favourite nephew of hers, which he suspected, in a humorous sort of way, was because he had a good clear voice – perfect material for her experiments. He made his request from one end of a large room while she listened to him with the various models at the other end. At length, he made himself sufficiently audible and his request was granted, and he arranged things with Tim, her chauffeur.

Early next morning, St Donat's was in a state of pandemonium, and after the last-minute preparations had been attended to, the boys, in twos, threes, and in laughing, jostling groups, set out on the first stage of their trip to the railway station in Abbeymead. Soon the little travellers were out of sight, and their merry voices gradually died away in the distance. David, who had been watching them from the steps outside the main building, was feeling very disappointed. He had been so looking forward to the outing, but he had kept up a cheerful front while wishing his friends a good day's fun. He was surprised to see Richard De Macey coming towards him when everyone else had gone.

'Hello, Richard! Aren't you going to Cambridge?'

'Not just yet,' Richard replied awkwardly, sitting down on the steps. He had got all the fiats that were necessary for David to go with him, including Dr Gillespie's, on condition that his patient took things easy and didn't injure his ankle further, which all the sightseeing perambulations around Cambridge might have done. However, he had yet to broach the subject with David himself, and he was feeling just as embarrassed as he had been in the Headmaster's study the evening before.

'You'd better hurry. The others must be halfway to Abbeymead by now.'

'I've plenty of time, David,' was the baffling answer, which left David very puzzled indeed.

An old but very elegant limousine, its bodywork gleaming from frequent and loving care, glided almost silently towards them up the drive and came to a smooth halt a short distance from where they were talking.

'What a beautiful car!' exclaimed David, his admiring eyes busily examining it from front to rear bumpers. 'I wonder who owns it?'

'Some rich old lady with more money than sense,' Richard replied, smiling, and they both laughed.

The uniformed driver came over to them. 'Are you ready to go, Master Richard?' he asked.

'In about ten minutes, Tim.' He caught David by the arm. 'Come on, David. Let's go upstairs so that you can get ready. It's too good a day to waste any of it.'

'But …' began the bewildered David.

Richard was now in full command of the situation, and his awkward embarrassment was gone.

'But me no buts,' he commanded with a laugh. He helped David indoors and on the way up to the dormitory explained the position to him. 'And my aunt told me that I could have Tim and her car for the day,' he concluded, 'so you won't miss a day's outing after all.'

'Thank you, Richard,' David replied, a lump rising in his throat at the other's thoughtfulness.

Richard squeezed his arm.

'We'll get to the Broads just as soon as they get to Cambridge, and we'll see much more of the countryside by car than they will by rail as we go along.'

David enjoyed the drive, and as they sat in the spacious luxury of the back seat he excitedly followed his companion's pointing finger. Richard knew his native Norfolk well and made an excellent cicerone, pointing out objects of interest along the way and naming the pretty olde-worlde little villages and telling many an amusing or historic anecdote associated with them. When they reached their destination, Tim unpacked a picnic basket, which contained flasks, fruit, sandwiches and various dainties – it was very enjoyable eating out in the fresh air on the grassy bank of a waterway on a beautiful, warm and sunny day.

'David,' said Richard suddenly during the course of their

conversation, after Tim had left them to themselves, in a voice that had gone strangely hoarse, 'will you be friends with me in future?'

'You know I will, Richard,' David answered, nodding his head, and Richard breathed a sigh of relief and contentment. He had accomplished successfully what he had set out to do.

After they had stowed away a considerable quantity of eatables, the two new friends lay on their backs on the grass and gazed up idly at the blue dome of the heavens as they talked. When the sun was beginning to set, in a sky that looked as if it was composed of innumerable rubies, Tim returned to drive them back to the Abbey. It had been a wonderful day for both of them, and a noteworthy one, too, for each had made a special friend.

26

David Visits Richard's Home

The friendship between Richard and David ripened more and more, and soon all of David's intimate friends – including Tony and Arthur – were Richard's also. At David's and Tony's invitation, Richard moved to their corner in the study, and although it was a crowded one, it was a happy one and became a meeting place for the boys of Abbot's whenever there was anything to be discussed *januis clausis*, in a manner of speaking.

Owing to certain alterations that had to be carried out in the wing of the Abbey where the classrooms were, the boys were given a break of four days, and those whose homes were within a convenient distance of the school were allowed to spend the short, fortuitous break with their families if they wanted to.

Richard decided to avail of the opportunity. David helped him pack a few things, and when they had finished this they went down to the study to wait for Richard's father, who was coming to drive him home. They were passing the time by asking riddles when there was a knock on the door.

'That must be him now,' Richard said, rushing over to the door to let him in.

Sir Frederick had motored down from Norfolk in a gloomy frame of mind. He had come to the heartbreaking conclusion that he would never experience a father's pride in his son, for since the previous summer the gulf between them had widened considerably, and when he had seen him last, Richard had still appeared to be making no effort to mend his ways. Before seeing his son now, he had called on Dr Princeton to discuss the problem with him, and what the Headmaster had to say about Richard's complete personal reorientation was something, in his wildest imaginings, he had never expected to hear.

Richard went up to him shyly and, taking the initiative, stood up on tiptoe and kissed him on the forehead. His father thought to himself that this small act alone would have been sufficient in itself to amply repay him for his journey from Norfolk.

'This is David Madison, my best friend, Father,' Richard disclosed, introducing David.

Sir Frederick took his hand and gave it a friendly squeeze.

'I'm very pleased to meet you, David.' He observed, with satisfaction, that this new companion of his son's was everything that he might himself have picked for him. He was completely won by his naturalness and quiet charm. 'Haven't we met some place before?'

'No, sir.'

'You saw him when you were here during the spring term, Father,' Richard said, blushing at this reminder of that painful meeting. 'He was with Tony Masefield.'

'Yes, I remember now.' Sir Frederick recalled how his son had referred scathingly to David as a scholarship boy at the time. The fact that Richard was now a friend of his was in itself an eloquent indication of how greatly he had changed his views.

Later, when father and son were alone together, they had a very intimate chat, the first that they had ever really had with each other.

'That's a very fine boy, Richard. Tell me about him. I'd like to hear about how he has got on here.'

Nothing loath, Richard began at the beginning and traced his career since he had come to St Donat's, with all its trials and tribulations. He did not omit the part that he had played in it, both good and bad, and his father listened with a very sympathetic ear.

Sir Frederick noticed that the change in his son was very

obvious, and he was pleased to see that he had completely dropped that haughty, overbearing manner which he had previously adopted. He was also more relaxed in his ways, and seemed more of a child than he had been and showed a new, filial dependence on his parent which both of them found satisfying.

'David is the kind of boy that your mother and I would wish you to be friends with, one who has proved himself against the odds. Remember, Richard, no matter what sort the company is, a person is bound to take his example from it and accept its particular standards as being the norm, for good or ill. You're not the same boy as you were before. You've grown up in character, and at the same time you're younger in many respects than you were. Wisely, you have learned from your experiences here this past year and have had the good sense to profit from them. Your manliness in admitting to your mistakes is something that makes me very, very proud of you.'

Richard's eyes met his father's in perfect communion.

They met Mr Ledwidge in Cloister Court, and he mentioned Richard's progress in his studies.

'You have made me very, very happy, Richard,' his father said, when the teacher had left them. 'I was perfectly satisfied with your change in attitude, but this report of Mr Ledwidge's crowns my pleasure. Is there anything special that you'd like? I don't think that I could refuse you anything at this moment.'

'May I invite David home with us?' Richard asked, without a moment's hesitation.

His father smiled at him.

'You are always quite free to invite the right kind of boy for a visit. I'd be delighted to have him stay with us.'

Richard was pleased at the way David had impressed his father, for it was evident that he had taken an instant liking to his new friend. He rushed off to find him and, needless to remark, David was thrilled with the invitation. It didn't take them long to get his small suitcase packed, and they soon joined Sir Frederick, who was waiting for them in his car.

After a light meal in Abbeymead, they set off for Norfolk. They made a detour to Ipswich, in Suffolk, in the early afternoon, Sir Frederick having some business there, and about an hour or so later they reached the end of their journey, enjoying the beautiful rural countryside of the two counties on the way. Lady De Macey came out of the house to greet them. She guessed intuitively that past differences between her husband and their son had somehow been interred, and she was just as struck by the obvious change in Richard as her husband had been before her.

'Show David to the guest room, Richard,' she said, after David had been introduced to her and they were inside the house. 'We'll have dinner when you come down. The pair of you must be famished after your trip.'

David was awestruck when he saw how immense the inside of the house was. And the guest room! He was sure that it was at least half the size of his own home. The large windows, which overlooked the flower garden, were open, and the rich fragrance of roses and carnations and other seasonal flowers pervaded the room. His case, which a maidservant had taken from him on their arrival, had been unpacked, and his pyjamas were neatly folded on the large bed.

'How do you like the place, David?' asked Richard, enjoying his pleasurable reaction to it.

'It's ... it's wonderful, Richard. I've never seen such a beautiful house and gardens. They're just like a picture in a book.'

That night Richard enumerated all the things that they would do during the following four days, and David dreamed about the schedule when he fell asleep. The following morning he was given a tour of the house and grounds, and Richard recounted the many historical facts and legends which were connected with his home. The grounds of the estate were particularly attractive to a city-reared boy. David would have liked to have stayed in the flower garden all day to enjoy the gorgeous blooms, but there were so many other sights to be seen and things to do and he was determined to miss nothing.

After lunch, Richard showed him the stables.

'I'll teach you how to ride, David,' he announced briskly, much to his friend's delight, since he had never been on a horse before.

Richard led two ponies from their stable into the yard and paraded them up and down in order to display their good points.

'You can learn on Chestnut.' This was the smaller of the two ponies with a long, flowing mane and a white tail. 'He's as quiet as a lamb, and he never rears or kicks. See, he likes you already' – the pony was nuzzling David's chest. 'Which way would you like the stirrups?' he asked, after he had put the saddle on. 'High like a jockey's, or low like a cowboy's?'

'I think I'd like them low,' David answered, his decision being based on the assumption that the more his legs were astride his mount the less chance there would be of losing his seat and falling off.

Richard made the necessary adjustments and then helped him onto the saddle. In spite of the assurances concerning Chestnut's docile nature, David sat as rigidly as he could and was almost afraid to breathe in case the pony became frightened and bucked. Richard mounted his own pony and led Chestnut by the reins into a field where he showed his pupil the basic rudiments of horsemanship. After a while, he allowed David to ride in a wide circle, while he stood in the centre holding a rope that was attached to the pony. David gained more and more confidence as the lesson proceeded, and the little knocks to his face which he received now and then from Chestnut's bobbing head became less frequent as his balance improved. Richard had not been exaggerating, for Chestnut was as quiet as a lamb, and both pony and rider hit it off admirably together.

After the lesson was over, the two boys went for a swim. A river ran through the estate, so they changed into their swimming trunks in the house and dried themselves there after their dip. That evening, after dinner, they played billiards with Sir Frederick. The baronet was quite a good player, as was his son. David had never played the game before, but being naturally dexterous, he took to it like a duck to water and distinguished himself by making a few presentable – albeit lucky – breaks. And so to bed after a light supper – but not to sleep immediately – for the two friends talked on and on in David's room till tired tongues could wag no more and Richard went back to his own bedroom.

On the third day of their short break, a very unpleasant incident occurred. When David was in the stable yard saddling his pony, Richard, who had been collecting some riding tackle in the house, met Gilbert Roye coming up the drive.

'Hello, Richard!' Gilbert said, with his usual self-satisfied smugness. He had apparently recovered from the indignity of what had been tantamount to an expulsion from St Donat's.

'What do you want?' demanded Richard, frowning darkly at him.

'Will you come to my birthday party during the holidays. 'There'll be lots to eat and plenty of fun. My mother says that it will be the best children's party in the county this year. There's a magician coming from Norwich to entertain us.' This last piece of information was disclosed in the hope of acting as an irresist-ible inducement.

'If he makes you disappear, he'll be worth every penny he's paid,' Richard growled. 'I don't want to go to your party, no matter how good it is, and I don't want you calling here again.'

David appeared leading his pony. On seeing the unwelcome visitor, he stopped uncertainly.

'What's he doing here?' Gilbert asked, jerking his head in David's direction and scowling at him.

'It's none of your business, but, if you must know, my father invited him, and I can invite him as often as I like.'

The other sneered.

'You'd think the little tramp had no home of his own to go to.

Your father must have taken pity on him.' With his customary vindictiveness, he was trying to cause David as much pain and embarrassment as he could.

'You'd better clear off before I lose my temper,' Richard threatened menacingly, moving in his direction. Gilbert beat a cowardly retreat down the drive, mumbling incoherently to himself as he went. 'I'm sorry, David. I never imagined that he'd ever dare to show up here again.'

David was looking very downcast and his face was flushed.

'I don't want to be the cause of any trouble between you and him, Richard.'

'He's no friend of mine anymore, David, and you're my best one. If anyone insults you, he insults me, and that's the way it will always be.' The subject was closed as far as he was concerned, and he vaulted on to the saddle of his pony.

His father came out of the house and, seeing his son already mounted, caught David under the arms.

'Ups, David!' he said and swung him up onto Chestnut's back.

The boys left him and went cantering over the green fields, the unpleasant intrusion forgotten.

Too soon the short break came to an end, and David was a little sad because he had enjoyed every minute of it. Sir Frederick drove them back to school. His last words to David before he left them were: 'There'll be many more holidays, David, and it will always be regarded as a great pleasure by Richard's mother and myself if you spend part of them with us.'

27

The School Year Comes to an End

The last few weeks of the summer term were happy ones for David and his three friends, and their cup was full when, under Thornley's masterful captaincy, they won the cricket competition. They went on many tramping expeditions together and explored every nook and cranny of the beautiful Essex countryside around the Abbey. The four boys were well matched. At his books, David had no peer; at rugby and cricket, Richard was the acknowledged master; Arthur's claim to singularity probably rested upon his precocious sapience; as for Tony – well, Tony was Tony – he was the life, soul and heart of the little group, and with his hot temper and fluent invective – which often got him into unpromising situations – he always kept his friends amused and entertained.

Relations, too, between the quadrumvirate could not have been more harmonious. As mentioned elsewhere, David seldom quarrelled with anyone, let alone his friends; Arthur was too emotionally stable to allow trifles to come between them; and Tony, despite his quixotic propensity to tilt at windmills in other quarters, never fell out with David or the others. Richard, however, with his sparkling, mercurial personality, was prone to sudden, cruel disaffections, particularly where those he loved best were concerned. Since he and David had become so close it was inevitable that an occasional rift would occur between them. Such a one occurred on one of the last afternoons of the term.

To celebrate the approach of the holidays, the boys of

159

Abbot's, intoxicated with their recent success in cricket, challenged some of the senior boys to a game. Thornley captained the junior side, as usual, and won the toss, and he sent Richard and Tony in for the first innings. Richard strolled majestically over to the wicket.

'Watch me, David,' he shouted airily over his shoulder. 'I'll give the bowlers a punishing that they'll never forget.'

'Don't count your chickens before they're hatched, Richard,' David, who was sitting outside the pavilion, cautioned with a laugh.

Richard made a great fuss about seeing that the wicket was just right. He evidently anticipated a long innings.

The Captain of Higher School – a strapping young fellow named Brown – was bowling and took his measure shrewdly. He had a healthy respect for Richard's batting prowess, and he had no intention of bowling in a slipshod way because of the age difference between them. With tremendous energy, he sent the ball down the hard, dry pitch and it broke sharply off a well-placed spinner. Before Richard knew what was happening, bails and stumps were flying in all directions. He looked behind him in utter bewilderment and disbelief. He just couldn't believe his eyes. He made such a ludicrous picture that there was a spontaneous roar of laughter from both teams.

'You haven't been bowled, Richard,' David shouted, 'it's only your imagination.'

There was a fresh roar of laughter from the highly amused boys at this humorous remark. With a disgusted expression on his face, Richard shouldered his bat and left the field. David followed him into the pavilion.

'I've never seen anything so funny,' he commented, laughing.

At any other time, Richard would have laughed as well, but he was in one of those irritable little tempers when it was a pleasure to hurt the ones he loved.

'I didn't think it was funny,' he said coldly, frowning in vexation.

Not wishing to upset him further, David stopped laughing. 'You're not angry with me, are you?'

'For heaven's sake, go away and leave me alone,' Richard replied roughly, relishing the hurt that he was causing.

'But, Richard …' persisted David, putting a hand on his shoulder.

Richard brusquely shook it off and, pushing past him, left the pavilion. David hesitated, but did not follow him. He was never responsible for falling out with him and any offence he might have caused had been completely unintentional.

As for Richard, the perverse pleasure he had felt at wounding a gentle heart lasted for only a short period. After that, he smothered a sense of guilt by fanning a grievance which he was pleased to think was the result of a slight to his dignity. When David came up to the dormitory that night with Tony, he pretended to be asleep – a pretence which fooled no one – and the feeling of pleasure at hurting his friend returned once more. David undressed and got into bed without saying anything, but Tony could not refrain from making a remark about him:

'What's wrong with crosspatch, David? Has he lost his horrible little temper again?'

David did not reply, and Richard gritted his teeth to refrain from making an angry retort that was on the tip of his tongue at this piece of insolence. Tony winked at David. 'It's just as well that he's asleep. It's the decent thing for him to do when he's like that.'

David smiled at his facetiousness and several boys who were listening began to titter, but not too loudly, however, in case the bear with the sore head directed an attack in their direction for taking liberties.

They didn't even say goodnight! Richard fumed illogically, disregarding the fact that he was supposed to be asleep, not just lying more or less doggo.

By the following afternoon he was beginning to find the separation unbearable. He knew that he had been in the wrong and that it was his business, not David's, to eat humble pie and make the first overtures.

When he sought Tony's help, Tony refused point-blank, as he always did, to act as a mediator.

'You must suffer the consequences of your rash temper and apologize like a man,' he reprimanded severely. 'It's all your own fault, and it would serve you jolly well right if David never spoke to you again.' Tony knew how to punish him where it hurt most.

Such a possibility was frightening, and Richard vowed to himself that he'd never act so hastily again – that was, if he were forgiven this time. He summoned up his resolve and went to look for David. He couldn't find him anywhere, and as the hours flew by he became anxious. David had simply disappeared into thin air. He met Arthur outside the bicycle shed.

'Hello, Arthur!' he said, and then asked with an air of assumed indifference: 'Where is he?'

Arthur had been told by Tony about what had happened, and, like Tony, he never sided with Richard when he was in the wrong. In order to punish him a little for yesterday's churlishness, he feigned ignorance of his query.

'Where's who?' he inquired, a feigned expression of puzzlement on his bespectacled countenance.

Richard realized the reason behind his obtuseness and curled his lips in chagrin.

'David, of course.'

Arthur sat on the crossbar of his bike.

'You'll see him after the holidays – *if* you're lucky,' he said, rubbing it in.

'What do you mean?' Fear and apprehension had gripped his listener's heart.

'David's in sickbay. He got sick after lunch.'

'Then I must see him at once.' Richard was very much chastened by this, and, although the sun was still warm, the day seemed to have suddenly become cold.

'You can't!' was the solemn dampener, delivered with a grave shake of the head. 'He's got a rash, and Matron is treating him as an infectious case. He's in isolation and no one is allowed to see him.'

'It's not serious, is it?' asked Richard anxiously.

'I wouldn't say so.'

'That's good, anyway.' Richard was relieved by this assurance and dismissed lurid thoughts of ambulances and operating tables from his mind. 'But I've got to see him, Arthur, otherwise he won't come to Norfolk for a visit during the holidays.'

'"The best laid schemes o' mice an' men gang aft a-gley", Richard, and you should know by now how hard David takes it when you fall out with him.'

'I'll never fall out with him again.'

Richard was now very distressed and Arthur decided that he had punished him enough.

'Father doesn't think that he's got an infectious fever. He hasn't seen him yet, but I told him the symptoms and signs. Anyway, he's probably had all of the fevers already.'

'Then what's wrong with him?'

'He got sick after eating those shellfish that Thornley produced at lunch. He may be allergic to them.'

After Arthur had gone careering down the drive on his bike, Richard went to see Matron, with the hopeful intention of seeing David to make it up.

'Well, young man, what can I do for you?' asked that buxom lady briskly, scanning him expertly for signs of injury or illness.

'I'd like to see David Madison, Matron,' he requested, with his most disarming and winning smile.

'He's in isolation until the doctor sees him. You'll have to wait until then, dear.'

Taking a deep breath, Richard played his trump card, which he had been holding up his sleeve in the event of a refusal, and told her Arthur's diagnosis.

'That might well be so,' she replied cheerfully, 'but until the *real* doctor sees him, there he stays.' It was likely that she had before her mind a similar type of case which hadn't quite fitted in with the books and, consequently, she was taking no risks.

Richard had to be satisfied with that, and he retired crestfallen.

David was discharged from sickbay the next day. Arthur had been right in his diagnosis, and a few tablets took care of the condition. Richard inquired solicitously about his health and then apologized to him with great humility and swore undying loyalty in future.

On the eve of the last day of term Dr Princeton and his wife gave a farewell dinner in their house in honour of Brown, the Captain of Higher School, who was leaving that year; and in keeping with the usual custom of the school, a representative number of boys were invited. Thornley, as Captain of Lower School, was there, of course, and David was both surprised and delighted when he was asked to represent Abbot's House, a gesture, which he learned later, had been proposed by Mr Ledwidge and approved by the Headmaster.

It was a quietly moving occasion, with an underlying note of sadness. The Headmaster delivered a short address, and he was followed by Mr Ledwidge and some of the other masters. Thornley spoke, as well, a blundering, bashful, awkwardly phrased little oration that, nevertheless, came deep from the heart. He was so overcome with emotion that he was unable to finish it, and with a hurried 'Godspeed!' he sat down in confusion. David thought that it was the most wonderful speech of the evening, and the volume of the applause that succeeded it indicated that he was not alone in his judgement of it. Brown then replied and briefly mentioned how much he owed to the Abbey and its teaching staff; and he ended up by saying that he would never forget the school after crossing the threshold into manhood and entering the wider world outside its gates.

The next day Dr Princeton and Mr Ledwidge bid the departing Captain a last farewell. He spotted David in the background and went over to him with outstretched hand.

'Goodbye, Madison,' he said.

'Goodbye!' replied David, a lump rising in his throat.

Abruptly, the Captain opened the door of an awaiting car, not trusting his emotions any further. Before he got in, he took one last, long look about him, then as abruptly got into the car and didn't look back again.

When he had gone, Dr Princeton and Mr Ledwidge began walking slowly back towards the school, with David between them. Each of the masters was busy with his thoughts, because it always affected them deeply to see their senior boys leave. At length, Mr Ledwidge spoke.

'He was a fine young fellow, Headmaster. He will certainly go far in the world. It's such a pity that we have to lose boys like him so quickly.'

'Yes, Mr Ledwidge,' was the slow reply. 'He was one of the finest Senior Captains we've ever had.' The Doctor clapped a hand on David's shoulder. 'It will be quite a few years before we lose you, eh, Madison?'

'Yes, sir,' replied David with an emphasis that he couldn't hide, looking up at the two men who were smiling down at him. To him, the future stretched out ahead like an endless age, but to the two adults, from their perspective of time, he would be leaving all too soon.

Tony Masefield had set off for his home in Suffolk that morning, after bidding a sad goodbye to his friends, and late in the afternoon Sir Frederick De Macey came to collect Richard.

'See you in July, David,' were Richard's parting words, referring to the invitation to his home which he had given him a short time after his friend's brief illness.

David waved after them, drinking in the peace and calm of a beautiful evening. Few boys remained in the school, and an unusual quiet reigned about its age-old precincts. High above, the clock was chiming the hour, and David looked upwards with shining eyes. Then, with a happy smile, and filled to overflowing with joy and boyish optimism, he ran towards the main entrance of the Abbey, ran through the hallowed corridors inside, ran across Cloister Court, ran through Great Cloister and Cloister Passage, and didn't stop running until he was in Abbot's House.